T0152694

FREEDOM TO LOVE

What Reviewers Say About Ronica Black's Work

"Ronica Black's debut novel *In Too Deep* has everything from nonstop action and intriguing well-developed characters to steamy erotic love scenes. From the opening scenes where Black plunges the reader headfirst into the story to the explosive unexpected ending, *In Too Deep* has what it takes to rise to the top. Black has a winner with *In Too Deep*, one that will keep the reader turning the pages until the very last one."—*Independent Gay Writer*

"...an exciting, page turning read, full of mystery, sex, and suspense."—*MegaScene*

"...a challenging murder mystery—sections of this mixed-genre novel are hot, hot, hot. Black juggles the assorted elements of her first book with assured pacing and estimable panache."—*Q Syndicate*

"Black's characterization is skillful, and the sexual chemistry surrounding the three major characters is palpable and definitely hot-hot-hot...if you're looking for a solid read with ample amounts of eroticism and a red herring or two you're sure to find *In Too Deep* a satisfying read."—*L Word Literature*

"Black is a master at teasing the reader with her use of domination and desire. Black's first novel, *In Too Deep*, was a finalist for a 2005 Lammy…With *Wild Abandon*, the author continues her winning ways, writing like a seasoned pro. This is one romance I will not soon forget."—*Just About Write*

"The sophomore novel by Ronica Black is hot, hot, hot."
—*Books to Watch Out For*

"Sleek storytelling and terrific characters are the backbone of Ronica Black's third and best novel, *Hearts Aflame*. Prepare to hop on for an emotional ride with this thrilling story of love in the outback. …Wonderful storytelling and rich characterization make this a high recommendation."—*Lambda Book Report*

"This sequel to Ronica Black's debut novel, *In Too Deep*, is an electrifying thriller. The author's development as a fine storyteller shines with this tightly written story. …[The mystery] keeps the story charged—never unraveling or leading us to a predictable conclusion. More than once I gasped in surprise at the dark and twisted paths this book took."
—*Curve Magazine*

"Ronica Black handles a traditional range of lesbian fantasies with gusto and sincerity. The reader wants to know these women as well as they come to know each other. When Black's characters ignore their realistic fears to follow their passion, this reader admires their chutzpah and cheers them on…These stories make good bedtime reading, and could lead to sweet dreams. Read them and see."—*Erotica Revealed*

"Ronica Black's books just keep getting stronger and stronger. …This is such a tightly written plot-driven novel that readers will find themselves glued to the pages and ignoring phone calls. *The Seeker* is a great read, with an exciting plot, great characters, and great sex."—*Just About Write*

"Ronica Black's writing is fluid, and lots of dialogue makes this a fast read. If you like steamy erotica with intense sexual situations, you'll like *Chasing Love*."—*Queer Magazine Online*

Visit us at www.boldstrokesbooks.com

By the Author

In Too Deep

Wild Abandon

Deeper

Hearts Aflame

The Seeker

Flesh and Bone

Chasing Love

Conquest

Wholehearted

The Midnight Room

Snow Angel

The Practitioner

Freedom to Love

FREEDOM TO LOVE

by

Ronica Black

2017

FREEDOM TO LOVE
© 2017 By Ronica Black. All Rights Reserved.

ISBN 13: 978-1-63555-001-6

This Trade Paperback Original Is Published By
Bold Strokes Books, Inc.
P.O. Box 249
Valley Falls, NY 12185

First Edition: August 2017

THIS IS A WORK OF FICTION. NAMES, CHARACTERS, PLACES, AND INCIDENTS ARE THE PRODUCT OF THE AUTHOR'S IMAGINATION OR ARE USED FICTITIOUSLY. ANY RESEMBLANCE TO ACTUAL PERSONS, LIVING OR DEAD, BUSINESS ESTABLISHMENTS, EVENTS, OR LOCALES IS ENTIRELY COINCIDENTAL.

THIS BOOK, OR PARTS THEREOF, MAY NOT BE REPRODUCED IN ANY FORM WITHOUT PERMISSION.

CREDITS
Editor: Cindy Cresap
Production Design: Susan Ramundo
Cover Design By Melody Pond

Acknowledgments

This book is an example of what happens when a short story continues to grow and evolve. I just couldn't stop at 30,000 words!

A big heartfelt thanks to my Caitie, for reading at all hours of the day and night and simply telling me whether or not it was awful or doable.

Another thanks to the BSB team who still took this even though it went well beyond the short story proposed. Thank you all!

Cindy, as always, you rock. ;) Thank you for your continued support and belief in me.

For family. Blood or not. Love is love. Do it unconditionally.

Dedication

For my family in North Carolina…the true
definition of unconditional love.
I love you all.

CHAPTER ONE

Dare Creek County Correctional Facility
Dare Creek County, North Carolina

"Williams, move your ass." Mary Jo, an ancient prison guard, jerked Brynn to attention as if she could read her mind about somehow surviving the old concrete hellhole unscathed. She gave Brynn one last shove for good measure, knowing she wouldn't dare protest. She tossed Brynn's bag of belongings to her and signaled another guard to open the last locked door. Brynn held her bag full of goods from the canteen with one hand, while the other was tucked firmly behind her back. She knew it was a habit that would die hard, having been forced to walk that way for four years.

"Don't come back," Mary Jo said.

"Yes, ma'am." The door buzzed and Brynn stumbled through backward, nervous eyes still on Mary Jo. But as she walked out the final door, she smiled. No one was stopping her; no one was asking her questions or searching her.

She was free.

She pushed out into the press of new summer humidity. But damn, it felt good; free air was definitely different from confined. The bright sun was on her skin, the teasing heavy breeze playing with her hair. This was heaven. She closed her eyes for a moment taking it all in. Then she opened them and looked around.

The fences and the walls seemed enormous, and the grass beyond that, beyond the free road, seemed endless with hills of rolling green for miles. It was far different from the white glow of light she saw through smeared windows, or the fading scent of freshly cut grass as it crept over the walls. Rec time had been on cement, the sun slanting at an angle so you had to huddle in one area if you wanted to feel the rays and get a little vitamin D. A less restrictive cell block would've allowed her more freedom. But she'd been put where she was the most protected, and though she'd hated it, she was alive and unscathed and that was all that mattered.

She held out her arms and inhaled deeply. She could finally breathe without wincing from the smell of mold, body odor, and urine. She could not only breathe in the freshly cut grass, she could reach down and touch it.

Jesus H. Christ, it felt good.

"Well, don't just stand there," Mary Jo said from the open door behind her. "Go. There's no loitering here." Her hard face was crinkled with anger. She turned her head and spat tobacco as if Brynn had thoroughly gone and ruined her day.

"You'll be back," Mary Jo said. "Williamses always come back."

The words stung, but Brynn was used to them. She shrugged it off and bobbed on her anxious feet as a car pulled up along the main road. Large, rusted out, and loud, fumes billowed and the radio was so loud it was eating the speakers causing static. A hand rested on the doorframe holding a cigarette. It raised in a wave.

Brynn took off at a trot, then a jog, then a full-out run. Her jeans were loose from weight loss and her sneakers had seen better days. Her sister, Bea, was laughing as Brynn stopped at the car and yanked on her pants to keep them up.

"How ya doin', Sissy?" Bea asked, knowing she was irritating Brynn with her nickname. She looked her up and down and blew smoke through her nose. "Well, you're skinny, but you're alive."

Bea looked like hell herself with skin hanging off bones and dark dents beneath her wide eyes. By the look of her, no one would dare guess she was eight years younger than Brynn. A hard twenty-eight Bea was. And she looked as though she'd been drug by a horse through every single damn one of those days in those years. Her pupils told Brynn she was high and so did her laugh. It was loud, high-pitched, and wicked. She planted the cigarette in her mouth and leaned over to open the massive passenger door.

"Get in."

Brynn rounded the car, tossed her bag in the back, and climbed in. The door protested when it shut, and Brynn saw the wires hanging from the steering column.

"You pinch this car?"

Bea shrugged. "You said come get you. What did you expect?" She threw the car in gear and peeled out. Brynn thought about Mary Jo choking on the smoke and smiled inwardly. Instinctively though, she looked behind them, ready for the law to be right there on their ass. Thankfully, there was no one. She reached over and turned down the radio, preferring to hear the wind rushing at her rather than an old metal band.

"What happened to Papaw's Ford?" Brynn asked. Their grandfather had left them a nice F150 when he passed. They'd used that truck for everything.

"Traded it," she said, blowing out more smoke.

"What? For what?"

Bea didn't look at her, and Brynn knew whatever she was about to say was a lie.

"We had bills to pay. With you put away it hasn't been easy."

"Bullshit. All you had to pay for is power, water, and food."

"Yeah, well, a lot's changed, Sissy. You've been gone. So don't preach to me. I been doing what I can."

"Yeah, and let's not forget why I was locked up."

Bea flicked her cigarette out the window. "Don't start with me, Brynn. I didn't ask you to do it."

Brynn clenched her jaw, wanting to argue, to bite into her, but she held back. She held back just as she'd always done. "You didn't have to ask. And besides, you bawling like a baby...that was worse than asking."

Bea didn't respond and Brynn didn't push it. Her great-aunt had written a few times warning her of trouble at home. But a part of her had hoped Bea and Billy would get their shit together before she got out. But as usual, that was wishful thinking. And though Brynn had hated being locked up, honestly, it had been nice not having to take care of anyone. Imagine...discovering independence while locked up. Who would've thought?

Now she was free and she felt trapped again. Bea was driving her straight back into lock-down on Williams Lane. Brynn sighed and rubbed a suddenly aching temple. She'd kill for a Coke and a Goody's Powder, but it would be a while before a gas station. She settled back in the vinyl seat and stared ahead. Bea was still on drugs, snorting, smoking, maybe even selling. Who knew? Had Brynn going to prison taught her nothing? Hadn't it even scared her a little? It seemed not.

They drove for a long while, out into the country, pastures and rolling hills as far as she could see. Rolls of hay dotting the landscape here and there. But no people. Not a single damn one. She knew it should comfort her after being locked up like rats inside hell, but she felt a little panicked at all the open space. She willed her eyes to close, and as they did, she heard a distant siren. It was far away so she tried not to panic. But her brain fired off and she imagined them coming up behind, running the plate, pulling them over, throwing them up against the car, tightening those cuffs until they bit into their bones.

"Slow down," Brynn said, eyes still closed. She could feel Bea slow the car and the siren grow closer. When Bea's breathing changed, Brynn's eyes flew open.

"What is it?" she asked, turning in her seat to look behind.

"That SUV. It's coming up fast. Too fast."

Brynn saw the black vehicle bearing down behind them. "Fuck." She shrunk down in the seat and her heart nearly beat out of her chest. "Is it the law, undercover in one of those Tahoes? It could be, but there are no flashing lights in the grill."

"Here it comes," Bea said, gripping the wheel.

Brynn peeked over the seat and gasped with fear as the SUV nearly slammed into them. But at the last second, it swerved and flew past at an insane amount of speed. She watched it fly by and swerve back into their lane. Then her attention was behind them once again as the siren, which was incredibly loud now, came up on them going just as fast as the SUV. The police cruiser, lights flashing, siren wailing, was far from interested in their stolen car.

Brynn yelled at Bea "Get out of the way!"

Bea pulled off the road at full speed, allowing the cruiser to speed on. They watched, amazed and confused as their car bounced in the dirt shoulder. Suddenly, the SUV screeched and turned, facing the cruiser head on. The cruiser slammed to a stop just as shots rang out from the SUV. Pieces of glass flew up from the front of the cruiser, and Brynn could tell it was being hit with gunfire. The officers were trapped inside.

Brynn threw open the door as Bea screeched to a stop. "They're getting shot!"

"Brynn, wait!"

Bea reached behind the front seat and tossed her a handgun. Brynn didn't think, didn't process, she just lowered herself and ran toward the cruiser. Behind her, she heard Bea fire off a few rounds at the SUV.

Brynn kept moving. She could see two men hanging out the windows of the black vehicle. She fired two shots, hitting their windshield as she came to the back of the police car. She crab-walked up to the passenger door as each shot deafened her, causing her ears to ring. She looked inside and saw a male slumped behind the wheel, bleeding from a wound to the head, and another officer, a female, leaning to the left in the passenger seat. Brynn opened the door and the rounds continued to come from behind, from Bea, but they stopped from the SUV. Brynn tugged on the female's wrist. She moaned. Brynn climbed in and released her seat belt. Warm blood seeped into her T-shirt as she pressed against the officer. The woman was hit, somewhere in the upper shoulder area. Brynn reached out and pushed at the male. He didn't move and his shirt was torn with bullet holes.

"Shit." Brynn backed out and tugged on the woman again, sliding her from the car. When Brynn saw the blond ponytail and then her face, her mind flashed with recognition. It was Sergeant Vander, the officer who had arrested her for possession four years earlier. She had put Brynn in prison. But it didn't matter. She was shot and needed help. Brynn checked her pulse. Slow but steady. She heard the SUV peel out and speed away. Hoping it was safe, she half carried, half drug Vander back to their car. Bea stood still with her gun at her side.

"What are you doing?"

"We gotta get her to a hospital." Brynn was breathless and now covered in blood. "Help me get her into the car."

Bea didn't move.

"We can't do this, Brynn. We've already done too much." She walked over and looked at her face. "Shit, is that Vander? That bitch put you away, Brynn. Wanted me too. Do you know how much hell she's given me the past few years?"

"We can't let her die."

Bea turned away. "Not our problem. She's not our problem. We did our best. Now it's time to go. She's on her own. Which is more than she's ever done for us." She looked up and down the road, pacing. "What about the other one? I bet it's that son of a bitch partner of hers."

"I think he's dead."

"Shit." She grabbed her head. "Shit, shit, shit!"

"Bea, help me get her in the car."

"No. No way. I'm done." She tugged on her own hair in frustration. "We got a dead cop, Brynn. A fucking dead cop. You're soaked in blood; we both have guns. What the fuck do you think they're gonna do to us when they catch us? Give us awards?"

Vander moaned again in Brynn's arms. The blood was pulsing out of her.

"Fine. Stay here. I'll drive her myself." Brynn maneuvered Vander into the backseat and pulled a tank top from her bag of meager possessions. She folded it and pressed it into the wound. Vander winced and made a noise of protest.

"Shh, hang tough. We're getting you some help." Brynn was surprised at her own voice. It was calm, soothing. She was nurturing the cop just like she had everyone else in her life.

Bea climbed in behind the wheel, cussing and carrying on. She slammed the door shut.

"I'm not staying here with a dead cop," she said.

"Close the passenger door," Brynn said. "I'm staying back here to help her." Her mind was made up. Vander was not going to die on her watch. She pressed into the wound and supported her head. Vander stared at her as Bea closed the door and threw the car into gear.

"Williams?" she asked.

Brynn nodded. Vander tensed and started to panic, but Brynn held her hand and squeezed. "It's okay. We're going to the hospital."

Vander licked dry lips and her sky blue eyes focused. "My partner…"

"Shh, everything's okay. Just hang on."

"This is crazy," Bea said. "God damned crazy."

"Just drive." Vander was still watching her.

"My dog," she said and then swallowed. "He's home alone. If I don't make it…take care of him." Her breath shuddered, and Brynn stroked her face to calm her.

"He'll be fine. You'll be fine," Brynn said. Vander licked her lips again and nodded. A tear slipped down her face. Brynn had never noticed before how incredibly beautiful she was. Almost angelic with white-blond hair and pale eyes.

"Thank you," she said.

"Try not to worry," Brynn said. "It's all okay. You're safe."

Vander closed her eyes, and Brynn held her hand as Bea sped on.

"She gonna make it?" Bea asked, eyes looking in the rearview.

"If we hurry."

Bea gunned it, and Brynn held Vander in her arms, squeezed her hand, and watched over her as she fought for her life. Brynn did it all without an agenda or a second thought and wondered if she would return to prison the very day she was released. Maybe Mary Jo was right after all.

Chapter Two

Whit's her name?" Kat Vander turned her head
and opened her eyes. There was noise all around
her, and she wanted to fall back to peaceful sleep. A sharp
pain in her shoulder made her want to cry out, and her chest
and abdomen felt as though they'd been punched with brass
knuckles. A woman in blue scrubs was holding her hand
and touching her face, asking her to focus. She tried to look
warm, but Kat could see the deep lying seriousness.

"Vander…uh…Sergeant Vander," someone said to her
left. Kat moved her eyes to the woman gripping her other
hand.

"Williams?"

Brynn Williams, who was covered in blood, nodded.

What was a Williams girl doing here?

But there was no time to think or remember, for the
woman in scrubs was tapping her cheek.

"Sergeant, Sergeant, look at me."

Kat did.

"That's it. Focus on me, okay? My name is Harriet. I need you to try and stay awake." Harriet was joined by others dressed similarly, and they moved like bees swarming a hive. Kat realized she was the reason why.

She watched in silence as they stripped her and searched for other wounds. They were talking, shouting, poking, and prodding. Bullets, bullets, bullets. That was all they cared about.

Blood. It was all over her. Blood, they were shouting for it. Blood, it was brought in in a clear bag and hung on a pole. They poked. Blood in to replace blood out.

She wanted to tell them her blood type, but she was too weak to think, to talk. She looked back to Williams who had released her and was backing away. She held her gaze, wanting her to stay. Something about the look in her eyes. A focus, a determination. A will and a deep compassion. She never would've expected to see such a look on a Williams. Was she dreaming? Had she passed out? Regardless, she needed that look, those eyes, that tender hand. But someone escorted Williams through the curtain and she vanished.

Kat felt them lift and turn her to look for an exit wound in her shoulder.

More words and shouting. She felt cold now and tired. Warmth from somewhere deep was promised to her if she closed her eyes. She did so despite the voices asking her questions and giving her demands. The warmth came, gentle, soothing. The voices faded. Darkness closed in on the image she wanted to keep in her mind. The one of Brynn Williams willing her to live.

❖

"Kat, Kat?" Kat opened her eyes and winced in pain. Her shoulder felt like it had been knocked out of place. She moaned and tried to speak, but her throat was dry and sore.

"Here." A cup of water was pressed into her palm. She took hearty sips through a straw and shifted. She was uncomfortable. Numerous pillows were shoved behind her shoulder, putting her at an odd angle. Had someone mangled her shoulder? Were her bones out of place?

"Move the pillows," she managed, wincing again. "My damn shoulder hurts like hell."

She closed her eyes as a wave of dizziness overtook her. Nausea beckoned but passed.

"Kat, look at me."

Kat opened her eyes. This time she focused. Dave Murphy, a close friend and fellow cop, was sitting by her side along with his wife, Margie. Kat's heart pounded. Something was wrong. She only ever saw Margie at Thanksgiving and Christmas. And Murph, he looked scared shitless.

"What is it?"

Margie patted her leg. Kat looked down and saw that she was covered in a baby blue blanket. Another quick look around to her sides showed that monitors were keeping track of her vitals. She again looked to Murph.

"You've been shot," he said.

"Shot?" She swallowed hard. "Shot?"

A woman came in, wearing purple. She pushed buttons on a machine. "It's not unusual for her to be confused for a short while after the anesthesia. Don't be alarmed." And then she was gone, breezing through a curtain.

Margie took her hand. "You've just come out of surgery." Cream. Margie always reminded her of cream. Her skin was flawless and soft and shiny. Just like cream. The scent of White Diamonds permeated the air, and Margie pressed lipstick-covered lips together as she fought off tears.

"Shot?" Her slow mind tried to race, but it was moving through the sluggish marsh of what she could only guess was medication.

"In the shoulder," Murph continued. "But you're gonna be fine." He offered a smile. "You lost a lot of blood, but thankfully, you got here in time."

He adjusted his studious glasses, and Margie tossed her a smile as well. She glanced at them back and forth, studying. They were full of shit. They were trying to protect her. But from what, she didn't know. More pain registered and she checked under the covers, beneath the gown. She was covered in bruises. Looked like she had been beat to hell.

"Some of the bullets hit your vest," Murph said.

"Jesus, how many?" Her heartrate kicked up at the mere thought. *Why can't I remember?*

"Don't worry about that. Just worry about resting now. We'll get you some more pain meds as soon as you speak to your guys." Margie again patted her leg.

"They have some questions for you," Murph said. "Are you up for it?"

"Yes, of course. They'll tell me what's going on. They'll get me out of here." She tried to kick her legs over the side of the bed, but she was hit with dizziness and pain.

"Kat, stop it." Murph was standing, holding her back. "You're very weak."

She closed her eyes to stop the room from spinning.

Murph laughed softly. "Stubborn as always." He removed a pillow from behind her shoulder and she sighed with relief. "Better?"

She nodded.

She wanted to slug him, but she knew she couldn't.

"Elevate my arm a little more?" she asked.

He did so and she thanked him, opening her eyes to take in the two of them. Both were standing and they looked so Ma and Pa, Margie clutching her designer purse, well made up, and Murph in his camo ball cap and Polo styled shirt. He wiped a tear from beneath his glasses.

They bent and kissed her cheek. "We'll be right outside."

"Okay."

They left through the curtain, and her captain and a few other deputies rushed in. They looked pale with shock and their eyes were wide with panic. Her captain was wiping his brow.

"Captain, relax, they say I'm okay." He looked like hell. *What is going on?*

They all kissed her cheek and patted her hand. A few wiped tears.

"Fellas, it's okay." She searched their eyes and studied their posture. They weren't relaxing, and it was obvious everything was not okay.

Captain Bowman gripped her hand. "Vander." He cleared his throat. He was flushed so red she was worried he would pop.

"Cap, what is it?"

"You don't remember anything, do you?"

She searched her mind. "I know I was shot." And suddenly her heart dropped to her stomach. Her partner. Brian Damien. "Oh, my God." She clutched her gown at her chest. "Damien. Where is he?" She could see him, his body jolting with every bullet that hit him. He was trapped behind the wheel. She'd leaned over, tried to pull him down, but bullets tore into her as well, leaving her motionless. As she'd felt the hot blood pulse out of her body, she'd tried to release his seat belt. But then someone had been there, someone pulling her from the cruiser. A woman.

"He's been flown to Charter General," Captain Bowman said. "He's critical."

Kat felt tears nip at her throat. "Oh, Jesus."

"He's sustained multiple bullet wounds, one to the head, massive blood loss. They don't know if he's going to make it."

"I'm so sorry," she said. "It's my fault. I couldn't get him down. I couldn't get him down."

Captain Bowman squeezed her hand. "It's not your fault. I don't want to hear you blaming yourself. It won't do anyone any good." He wiped a tear and straightened. "Christ knows you did your best. All we can do is pray now." Silence hung in the air, and he cleared his throat and carried on. "We knew you were in pursuit of a stolen SUV. And from the footage we just viewed of your dash cam, we know they turned on you and opened fire. They ambushed you. You're damn lucky to be alive."

"What we can't see is what was going on behind you," a deputy she knew only as Chaz, said. He spoke softly, serious.

"Behind me?"

"Someone pulled in behind you and returned fire at the SUV. Someone pulled you from your vehicle and brought you here. All we got from the dash cam was an image of an older model Buick speeding away with what appeared to be two females inside. The plates came back stolen."

Kat looked away and scanned her mind. Kind, warm, hazel green eyes came to life. A gentle hand, holding her. A sweet voice, soothing her, telling her it was all okay.

"Yes," she said, almost to herself. "A woman."

Another deputy, a rookie she didn't know, raced into the room. "Captain, we just got the hospital security footage." He handed over an iPad and they gathered around. Captain Bowman looked up at her. "Do you know who it was, Vander?"

Kat could still see the face and the strands of auburn hair. The blood soaked T-shirt and the loose jeans. She could still see the look on her face. The one willing her to live.

"Yes," Kat said. "It was Brynn Williams."

The captain and the others continued looking, thumbing through more footage.

"This is outside in the emergency drop-off," the rookie deputy said.

Captain Bowman looked up at her in disbelief. "Bea Williams as well?"

Kat shook her head. "I'm not sure. I can only remember Brynn."

Captain Bowman brought the iPad to her. He showed her the footage of the old car speeding in, screeching to a stop, and two women pulling her from the car. One, Brynn, helped her inside, while the other, Bea, climbed back in and sped off.

"We know Brynn reported the shooting to the staff here at the hospital. She sent rescue, a chopper, after Damien.

But she wouldn't give her name, and she left soon after they began tending to you. At this time, we're having trouble locating either one."

"Apparently, she was just released from lockup today," Chaz said.

"Did she say anything to you, Kat? Anything that might help us find her?" Captain Bowman asked.

Kat's mind was spinning. *Just released? Shot at the SUV? Saved her? Sent them for Damien?*

"I have no idea. I don't know why they were there. Why they...helped."

Captain Bowman sighed, and she could see just how exhausted he was. But she knew his day was far from over. He'd go at it full force for days, they all would, until they found the SUV. "We don't either. But with their history and records combined, we're concerned they were somehow involved with the SUV."

"Which is why we need to find them. Talk to them," Chaz said.

Kat recalled the look, the touch. The soft words. "I don't think they were involved. The way...I just don't think they were involved. I don't think they'd risk themselves in helping me or Damien if they were."

"The plate on their vehicle came back stolen out of Winston Mills. Maybe we should start there," Chaz said.

Captain Bowman rubbed his forehead. "We need to speak to them regardless of your thoughts, Kat. The car they were in was stolen, and neither one is allowed weapons. They need to be brought in."

Kat felt her skin begin to burn at the thought of Brynn getting arrested the day she was released. All because she helped her. But the law was the law. If she could somehow see her, talk to her, she was sure she could work it all out.

"Cap, I want to talk to her." She tried to get out of bed, but the bunch of them all protested at once. "I want to be the one to bring them in. It should be me."

"Your only job right now is to recover. Let us do the rest."

He patted her hand and then nodded to the rest of the crew. "We'll be in touch." He paused, looked down at his feet, and then back up at her. "And, Vander? I'm glad you're okay." He left her bedside quickly, followed by the rest of them, and Kat watched helplessly as they went.

As she leaned back and closed her eyes, she, too, wondered why the Williams girls stopped to help. And more importantly, she wondered about the brave and tender way Brynn was with her. Just who was Brynn Williams and where in the world was she now?

CHAPTER THREE

G et in," Brynn said, screeching to a halt in a used
sedan. "Notice, this one isn't stolen."

Bea rolled her eyes and threw an Army duffel full of
clothes and gear in the back and climbed in.

"This is nice," Bea said, rubbing her hand along the soft
seat.

"It is, so let's keep it that way." Brynn sped away from
the old Sunoco gas station overgrown with kudzu. It had always been their go-to spot when they'd needed to meet up
and couldn't communicate. Now they were risking it all by
driving back down the road that led to the turnoff to their
home. But Brynn needed highway access, and the faster they
drove, the less likely anyone on their front porch would be
able to tell it was them in the blue Buick.

"Where the hell are you going?" Bea asked, lighting a
cigarette. She was sweaty, hands shaking. She tugged hard on
the cigarette, inhaling deeply before exhaling, but it seemed
to do little to relax her.

"Get down," Brynn said, slipping on large shades to hide her face.

Bea sank into the seat and they sped past their road and beyond old farmhouses with people relaxing in their porch swings, waiting for the afternoon storm. No one waved or even looked twice.

"Okay, you can sit up." Brynn pulled onto the highway and slowed to just above the speed limit. Bea shook her head, still confused. She knew where they needed to go to hide, and they were going the wrong way.

"Brynn," she said, demanding an answer.

"There's something I have to do."

"Yeah, what?"

Brynn wiped sweat from her own brow and checked the mirrors for the law. The car was a friend's, one who owed her many favors. Brynn had called Holly from near the hospital and she'd come to get her. She'd also given her clothes and supplies to escape with, not to mention the car.

"I made a promise," Brynn said. "And as you know, I keep my promises."

Bea made a noise of disapproval. "Cops are all over the family. Searched the property. Billy says they even found the old deer stand. As if we'd be dumb enough to hide in that."

"I'm not surprised." Neither one of them had been able to return home for fear of the police. Brynn had considered just turning herself in, but she didn't trust the police to do anything in her favor, and her fear of returning to prison had won out. Right now, she was just hoping Vander would live, and beyond that, she hoped she'd help clear her name. In the meantime, they needed to hide, and Brynn couldn't argue, knowing another charge on Bea would put her away for a long time.

"I got rid of the guns," Bea said.

"Where did you get them to begin with?"

She shrugged. "I don't even remember. Robbie or someone."

"Great." Robbie was a well-known druggie and, unfortunately, Bea's close friend. They'd known him since he was a kid, raising hell at age nine. Adulthood hadn't changed him a bit.

Brynn gripped the wheel with panic still coursing through her. Blood was beneath her nails and embedded into the lines of her knuckles. She'd only had time enough to change clothes and take a quick rinse under the water. And despite worrying about her family and her sister and running from the law, her mind kept returning to Vander and whether or not she was alive. She could still feel her warm blood, see her delicate blond lashes and pale eyes. There was so much life there in her eyes. Depths she was surprised to see.

She slowed as they approached the lake. She exited and found her way to a neighborhood near the water.

"Where the fuck are we going?" Bea demanded. She rolled up her window and once again ducked in her seat.

Brynn searched streets, then house numbers. She pulled over near her destination and examined the surroundings. Most people were still at work, and those that weren't were inside, hiding from the growing heat and humidity. Unlike in her neighborhood, where windowed air conditioners were weak and kept most on their porch praying for a breeze.

Bea looked around, and her face contorted in anger. She figured out where they were. Small towns kept very little private. And with Bea's doings, she probably knew where every cop lived and hung out.

"Tell me you're kidding," she said.

Brynn kept watch on the nice home, small in size but decent and on the water. A covered boat was in the driveway, along with a covered Sea-Doo.

"Stay here." She popped her door and took a step out.

Bea grabbed her arm. "Why the fuck are we at Vander's home?"

Brynn shook her off. "I told you, I made a promise."

She pushed out of the car, closed the door, and hurried across the street. She jogged to the back of the house where there was a large, elevated redwood deck and a lower level to the house she couldn't have seen from the front. She made her way to the lower level door and checked the knob. It was locked, but the door and knob were old, much like her own basement door. She dug in her back pocket and removed her wallet and a Costco card. She inserted the card into the door-frame at the knob and popped the door. She listened for an alarm. Nothing. Darkness encased her as she entered, along with the smell of grease, paint, and must. Another Sea-Doo sat to her right, guts displayed, with tools and parts surrounding it on wooden workbenches. Another one was covered and farther back in the dark. In front of her, stairs and a door at the top. She tugged on a string and a light bulb popped on.

Squinting in the bright light, she planted her foot on the bottom step and noise came from the door above. She stopped and made out the pet door just before a dog pushed through, barking. Brynn backed away as the dog ran down the stairs and stopped, barking at her in high pitch. The German shepherd mix was brave but also afraid.

She cooed him and carefully sat on the concrete floor. She looked away from him and waited. Slowly, he quieted and crept toward her. She comforted him and rested her hands at her side, palms up. He stepped to her and pressed his nose to her jeans and then her hand, which caused him to whine. She knew he smelled Vander, and she felt for him. She touched him and he licked her, first her hand and then her face.

She stood and clipped him to a leash she saw on a bench. He followed her back out the door, which she locked behind her.

"Good boy." She glanced around quickly, checked his name tag, and moved back to the side of the house where she stopped and looked for people. When she was satisfied, she hurried back to the car, dog in tow.

Bea was cussing before she even got the door open to put him in the back.

"A dog? A God damned dog? Brynn, have you lost your mind?"

Brynn climbed in and put the car in gear. She drove slowly down the street and found her way back to the entrance of the highway.

"If Vander dies, there's no telling how long he would be left in that house."

Bea shook her head. "Motherfucker."

"No, actually, I think his name is Gunner."

"Is he a fucking cop? One of those K-9 dogs? You know, attack on command and sniff out drugs?"

Brynn looked at him in the rearview mirror. He was sitting and panting.

"I don't know. He is a German shepherd."

"Fuck." Bea propped her elbow on the door and rested her head on her fist.

"He might be good to have around. You know, alert us to people."

"Yeah, and he might tackle me when I light up my pipe."

Brynn grimaced. "Even after I went to prison for you… and not to mention we're running from the law…you bring drugs?"

"I can't live without it. It fucks me up bad to go without. People like you just don't understand." She dug into her pocket. "But don't worry. I'm getting into downers now." She popped a few pills in her mouth and forced a swallow. "This will help calm me down."

"My God, how much did you just take?"

"Relax, I've got a tolerance now. What I just took, won't even hardly touch me. And it's expensive. Which is why I have this." She dug in the other pocket and pulled out a small rubber balloon. She smiled. "Know what this is?"

Brynn looked away. "Fuck off. I don't want to know. And wipe that damn grin off your face. You have no reason to be proud."

"Maybe not proud, but this right here, makes me very, very happy." She slipped it back into her pocket and leaned against the seat in a relaxed pose. She closed her eyes. "Wake me in a few or when you hit a gas station. I need a Mountain Dew."

Brynn accelerated, anxiety building. She knew what was in the balloon. A good number of women in prison were addicted to it. And the walls of the prison didn't seem to stop them from getting it. Fucking heroin. People were using it instead of the costly pills. Opiates were opiates. People didn't care about the form they came in, just the cost. And now Bea. God damn it. She might as well kiss her good-bye now. Heroin owned you and no one could seem to escape.

How had this happened? She was raised in the same house as Bea and Billy, and while it hadn't been ideal or even close to good, she'd never even considered drugs. Not after she'd seen what it had done to their parents and other family members. And she'd tried her best to raise Bea and Billy well, but it had been difficult with their parents partying before they passed, people in and out all day and night. But she had done her best. It just hadn't been good enough.

"And boy, have I paid the price," she said, causing Gunner to perk his ears. Next to her, Bea snored and the quiet allowed her to think of Vander. Giving Bea a careful glance, she plucked the pay as you go phone from her back pocket and dialed information. She connected with the hospital and waited, nerves on edge.

A woman answered with a sweet, deep Southern drawl.

"Yes, can I have Sergeant Vander's room, please?"

"One moment, please."

Brynn heard her typing.

"I'll connect you now. Thank you."

Brynn sat straighter. Another woman answered. Brynn hesitated, but only for a moment.

"I'm calling for Sergeant Vander," she said.

"She's resting and can't take calls."

"Resting? So she's okay?"

"She's in recovery. Who may I say is calling?"

"Her sister."

"She doesn't have a sister…Who can I say is calling?"

"Thank you, I just needed to make sure she was okay."

Brynn ended the call, heart racing. She was alive. She made it.

Brynn sighed with relief. Thank God. Now she just had to let her know about her dog. Hopefully, when she called again, she would be able to speak to her. Brynn cleared the call and returned the phone to Bea's pocket. She wouldn't understand the phone call or the need to check on Vander. Bea just wasn't made that way.

Brynn slowed and exited at a gas station. Instead of parking in the pavement lot, she parked in the field behind the building to avoid cameras. She gave Bea a rough shove and climbed out, opening the back door for the dog. He jumped out, happy to go explore. Brynn found him easy to walk. He heeled and listened well. After he finished his business, she returned him to the car, left the air on, and entered the store. She grabbed a Coke and some Advil and found Bea chatting up the cashier. Brynn got the feeling they knew each other.

Brynn put her goods on the counter and nudged Bea aside, giving her a look, letting her know she needed to shut her mouth. Brynn paid for them both and pushed out the door with Bea hot on her tail.

"What the hell, Brynn?"

Brynn kept walking, wiping fresh sweat from her brow. She climbed in the car and shut the door. Bea followed her with a pinched face.

"He's my friend."

"Doesn't matter. The last thing we need is you running your mouth, creating a trail."

Bea scoffed. "He won't snitch."

"Yeah, right. You better hope not."

Bea cursed and opened her Dew, nearly downing the whole thing. "You never believe me."

Brynn didn't answer, just pulled back on the highway. Bea was right. She never believed her, but there were a million reasons why.

"The cop lived," Brynn said to test her reaction. "Vander."

Bea stared at her for a moment, then shrugged. "So?"

"So, that's good. We did something good. We helped a cop. Saved her life." *Come on, Bea, care. Care about someone, something, anything.*

Bea belched. "What about the other dude?"

Brynn closed her eyes for a moment as a new sensation washed over her. Guilt. She should've checked him better. "I don't know. I'm not sure where they took him."

"Some place where they work miracles," Bea said. "That dude looked seriously fucked up when we drove past him. He looked dead."

"Yes." But that didn't mean he was. They should've taken him too. But she'd been too panicked, afraid. She'd just wanted to get out of there.

"I've never seen so much blood," Bea said. "They used him for target practice."

"Just shut up. Be quiet, okay?"

Bea kicked her feet up on the dash. "Grumpy."

Brynn rolled her eyes. "Gee, I wonder why. It's been such a fabulous day."

"Not my fault you wanted to play hero."

Brynn gripped the wheel, fighting the urge to backhand her. She'd never hit her; that was Uncle Mo's job. And he'd hit them all plenty enough. Didn't mean she didn't think about smacking her from time to time. Especially when she had attitudes like now.

"Bea. Shut up. Now."

Bea laughed but plucked out a cigarette and lit it. It occupied her and kept her from speaking, and Brynn relaxed a little. Gunner barked and Bea covered her ears.

"What the fuck?"

"Lower the window. He doesn't like the smoke."

"He's a dog."

"He still has to breathe, and frankly, so do I."

Bea lowered the window and he stopped and settled down. He groaned and Brynn smiled. She had finally found a companion.

Bea leaned back again and fell asleep, lit cigarette in hand. Brynn took it from her and tossed it out the window. She drove in peace for another hour and pulled off into the hills. The car bounced on the dirt roads, but she didn't slow. Gunner stood and she lowered the window for him. He hung his head and tongue out, enjoying the fresh air. Bea continued to snore, and Brynn wondered just what kind of tolerance she had for those pills. She checked her mouth for breathing and was satisfied for the moment.

Another half an hour on the dirt roads led her to the turnoff she needed. The car struggled but made it, and after another twenty minutes, Brynn was driving through over-grown brush off from the trail, until she stopped in front of the old cabin.

She gave Bea another shove, and she grumbled but didn't wake. Brynn left her, opening the door for the dog, who happily ran around. Brynn rounded the cabin, checking windows and what she could see of the roof. It hadn't been cared for in years, but it was still standing. She found a side window broken and pushed it open. A dank, dark smell rushed out at her.

"Damn."

She crawled inside and fell to the dusty floor. It took a moment for her eyes to adjust, but when they did, she found the front door, lifted the heavy slab of wood that served as a lock, and opened it. Light spilled in, and she could see the dust swirling all around her. She coughed and looked at the small living room, tiny kitchen, and single bedroom. Everything was dust coated and ancient.

Childhood memories flooded her, and she couldn't help but warm inside.

Gunner entered and sat, looking up at her.

"We got a lot of work to do, boy," she said, glancing out at the car where Bea remained asleep. By the look of her motionless arm and foot hanging out the window, Brynn knew it was less sleep and more passed out. She sighed and patted the dog on the head.

"Come on, let's go carry her inside."

CHAPTER FOUR

"Vander. Vander."

Someone was whispering and touching her softly. Kat opened her eyes, blinked heavily, and focused beyond her feet. Bright blooms of flowers saturated the room, and for a moment, she wondered what otherworldly place she was in. Oz perhaps?

"Hey," a voice came from her left. It was Murphy. He smiled, and she did her best to return it.

She closed her eyes and tried to recall where she was and why. The shooting rushed back, and she opened her eyes, panicked.

"Damien?" She gripped Murph's hand.

He squeezed. "He's recovering. It was touch-and-go for a while, but he's pulling through." He nearly whispered the last part, and she knew he wasn't telling her everything.

"Murph, what is it? What's wrong?"

He breathed deeply and released her hand. "Nothing. He's alive. You need to recover too."

She stared him down with her best "don't fuck with me" look, which usually left perps quivering in their boots. It usually worked on Murph too. But he was avoiding eye contact and rubbing his palms on his jeans. His firearm was on his hip, and the light blue polo he was wearing had darkened pools of sweat under his arms.

"It's not hot in here," she said.

He looked at her and took the bait. "No, it's actually very comfortable."

"Then why are you sweating like a rookie on his first day?"

Murph rose, crossed to the flowers, and looked at the notes. "You sure have a lot of people pulling for you. Praying for you. Damn near the whole county."

"Murph."

"And the food. Lord have mercy, the food. Margie and I have most of it, and a lot of the guys come by to check on you and to eat. I think I've gained ten pounds in the last few days alone." He touched his belly and smiled at her, but this time she didn't return it.

"Murph, what the hell is going on?"

"Doc says you're about ready to go. So you can join me and get a little fat as you recover. Margie says you need it. Says you're looking a little peaked. And I have to agree.

You need to eat, bulk back up. All that muscle needs fuel, and with you losing all that blood and not eating the hospital food—"

"That's it," Kat said, throwing back the covers and slinging her legs over the bed. "I'm getting out of here." She stood, winced at the pain, and remembered her shoulder. Her arm sat snug in a sling. She snapped at Murph, who was standing there, shell-shocked. "Hand me some clothes, will ya?"

He glanced around with a panicked look on his boyish face. Finally, he found a cabinet and retrieved a pile of folded clothes. He brought them to her and hitched his thumb.

"Margie brought them for you. Some of my sweat pants and old T-shirts." When she didn't respond he said, "I'm just going to go get a nurse or someone. I don't think they're ready for you to leave yet."

"You won't do any such thing." She glared at him and he dropped his hand and swallowed. "You say anything to anybody and I'll tell Margie about that hooker you have a thing for."

His face went pale. "I don't have a thing for her."

"Please," Kat said as she carefully pulled on a pair of sweatpants. "You blush redder than a thirteen-year-old boy caught with a porno mag when she talks to you."

"I do not."

Kat grinned. "Yeah, bud, you do. And we all know it."

He crossed his arms over his chest. "You're all a bunch of dicks."

She laughed. "Maybe. But we've got your number, Murph." Murph was a softie and everyone knew it. He was often the brunt of a joke, but it was because they loved him and looked after him. And there was no one better at talking to vics than Murph. And smart…holy shit was he smart. She wouldn't trade anyone for him, not in a million years.

She motioned for him to come closer. "Help me out of this sling and this gown."

He took a step and hesitated. "I really think a nurse—"

"Murph, get your ass over here and help me. Besides, I'm not Diamond, so seeing my breasts should do nothing for you."

"Dick. You're a dick, Vander."

"I know. Now help me." She turned so he could untie the gown and then turned again so he could help her out of the sling. When she was free, she tugged the gown forward and off and he blushed despite himself and looked away.

"Margie said a woman called while you were asleep. Said she was your sister."

"My sister?"

"Yeah, Margie said you didn't have one, and she just said she needed to make sure you were okay and hung up."

"Williams," Kat whispered, fighting a smile.

"Hmm?"

"Nothing. Help me put that T-shirt on?"

He nodded and helped her into it, avoiding her eyes and her bare breasts.

"Any idea who would claim to be your sister?"

She sighed. "Who knows? I'll check into it though."

"Probably just a reporter," he said.

She continued to dress. "Thanks. Now help me get the sling back on."

He did so and then helped her with the Adidas slip-ons. He packed up her clothes, along with her watch, necklace, and other belongings, and opened the door for her. Gently, he led her by the elbow and they smiled at passersby, including nurses. When they reached the elevators, he stopped.

"We better take the stairs," he said.

"Why?"

She was feeling a little weak, but she took a deep breath.

"Like I said, reporters."

"You're kidding?"

"Vander, this story is huge. Whole county's up in arms."

She followed him to the stairs and leaned on him all the way down. When they reached the bottom, she was sweaty and dizzy.

"Stay here," he said. "I'm going to go pull my car around back."

She nodded and leaned against the wall. Murph was right; she probably shouldn't be leaving, but damn it, he was keeping something from her. She needed to see Damien and she needed her own bed and...she looked toward the door, hoping for Murph. She needed information. All kinds of information. What all wasn't he telling her?

She opened the door and shuffled toward the back of the hospital. People stared, but she brushed them off. When she found a door that said no exit, she pushed through. Murph's white Dodge Challenger grumbled toward her, and he was cussing at her and rounding the car to open the door. She didn't hear a word he said, her mind too occupied.

He closed her door and slipped inside behind the wheel. He fastened both their seat belts and put the car in drive.

She looked at him point-blank. "Is Brynn Williams... okay?"

He slammed on the brakes but said nothing.

"Murph, fucking tell me. Tell me something. I'm dying here."

He sighed. "We don't know. We can't find her."

Kat leaned back and stared out the windshield at a darkening afternoon sky. Brynn had been the one to call and check on her; she was almost certain of it. It sparked warmth inside her, and she was desperate to know how she was, where she was. But Murph knew little, which meant Brynn was hiding out. She had an idea where, but she was too tired to think about it. Too weak to focus.

"She saved my life," she whispered and Murph drove on, to where, she didn't know, and at the moment, she didn't care.

Kat awoke as Murphy pulled in her driveway. She was groggy but still insistent, this time about Damien.

"I want to see Damien."

Murph sighed. "Another time, Kat. You can hardly walk as it is. Isn't it enough that I brought you home?" He didn't wait for an answer, just simply killed the engine and opened his door.

"Then tell me what you're hiding." Kat closed her eyes, fought light-headedness, and before she knew it, she was startled at Murph opening her door.

"Jesus, Murph, you're like a ninja." She waved him off and did her best to rise from the car. But halfway up she needed help, and Murph eased her to a stand without saying a word. She thanked him, hating that she needed the help. They headed toward the driveway door, Murph guiding her carefully while carrying her belongings.

"You just need to rest. I'll keep you updated on Damien. Right now, there's nothing new to report."

Behind them, a Chrysler 300 pulled in with Margie behind the windshield.

"You called her," she said, knowing Murph all too well.

"You shouldn't be alone."

"Says who?" But truthfully, she was grateful. She loved Margie, and Margie was an even bigger softie than Murph. Margie would be her ticket to Damien.

Kat turned again as another vehicle pulled along the curb. A news van. People spilled out, and a reporter was running straight for her. Thankfully, Margie headed her off, giving Murph time to unlock the door and help Kat inside. Immediately, she smiled and called for Gunner. When he didn't come, she felt her face fall and her stomach tighten.

"Where's my dog?" She looked to Murph and then Margie who entered and locked the door behind her.

"What's wrong?" she asked, reading her face.

"My dog. Where is he?"

They looked at each other in silence.

"You don't know?"

Kat tried to brace herself, but she was falling fast, and Margie and Murph helped her to her living room chair. She closed her eyes and rubbed her temple. Her heart was racing and she was sweating again. She desperately needed a pain pill, but she knew she wouldn't take it. She'd rather bite through the pain than have an opioid in her system.

"Maybe a friend has him?" Margie said.

Kat opened her eyes, Brynn Williams face in her mind. She'd asked Brynn to take him, but had she really done so?

Was she a woman of her word? Would she really risk everything to come get Gunner?

"I'm sure that's it," Kat said, no longer wanting to sound alarmed. She needed to talk to Brynn on her own to find out for sure. If she had been nice enough to care for Gunner, she didn't want her to suffer any trouble for it.

"I can make some phone calls," Murph said. "Go and get him."

Kat stood. "No. I mean, thanks, but I got it. Maybe a couple of days without him would be best right now. I'm not moving so well." She forced a smile.

She shuffled through her home, curious about Brynn's presence. What had she thought when she'd walked through? Where all had she gone? The living room was undisturbed and decorated in lakeside country charm with nautical blue walls, a cream-colored Clausen sofa, and sun washed tan grand chair. The reclaimed barn wood floors were antique softwood white. Her rug was Safavieh vintage turquoise. And most of her accents were beach woodcrafts she'd found on her visit to the coast. She loved decorating her home, and she found herself secretly hoping that Brynn had liked what she'd done. She continued to walk through, running her fingers lightly across her furniture, her thoughts lost in Brynn Williams and the idea of her presence.

She eyed the table in her kitchen and the last pile of mail she'd received. And her sink held a dirty coffee mug and a plate where she'd last had her egg whites and toast. She should've tidied up better, but she had been running late that morning, unaware that her life would be shortly changed forever.

Murph took her walking around as her needing something, and he searched her distressed white cabinets for a glass and poured her some juice. She waved it off, asking him to leave it on the table for later and headed for her bedroom. She knew it seemed silly, but thinking of Brynn in her home drew her there, and she stood and stared at her white duvet, blue distressed dresser and night table, and the large abstract painting she had hung above her bed. A half-empty bottle of water sat on her nightstand, along with a small stack of romance novels. Her skin warmed as she thought of Brynn thumbing through them. Not many people in town knew she preferred women to men, and she wondered what someone like Brynn would think. The thought stirred her inside in a way that she'd never felt before. Brynn possibly knew her secret. What would that mean? And how had it moved Brynn? Kat searched her mind, but she couldn't come up with a reasonable answer. She couldn't recall Brynn dating—ever. What did that mean? And more importantly, why did she care?

"Everything okay?" Murph asked, entering the room, hands in pockets. Despite trying to sound casual, he still looked worried. God bless him.

"Yeah," she breathed. "Great."

"I feel really bad about Gunner. To be honest, I forgot you had him."

Her stomach knotted with the anxiety of his whereabouts. It was something she'd have to see to soon. "He hasn't been with me long." She'd rescued him a year ago and had never been more in love.

"I stopped by," he said. "Checked the house. I should've noticed he was gone."

"When was that?" she asked, curious as to when someone took him.

"That first night."

She nodded, knowing then that it must be Brynn. There's no way Brynn would've known her condition until later. So she must've prepared for the worst and taken Gunner. "Can you do me a favor? Can you check all the doors and windows, make sure they're secure?"

He nodded and left her side, and she sat on her bed and rubbed her duvet. Sunlight streamed through growing clouds into her window to warm her, soothe her. Her eyes felt heavy and her stomach was growling for food. She wasn't used to feeling weak, to being down and out. She rarely took sick days, rarely relaxed with a movie on the couch. She spent her free time working on her Sea-Doos or out on the lake racing them, pushing them to their limits. And when she wasn't doing that, she and Gunner were out on long hikes or bike rides through the mountain trails. She liked to push her body, to push herself, to see how far she could go, just like she did with her Sea-Doos. Trouble was, she didn't know how to be under repair like her watercraft, various tools surrounding her, having dug into her and patched her back up. Unlike her watercraft, she had to heal, and the thought alone pissed her off.

"Murph." She stood and pulled back the covers on her bed. Like it or not, she needed to rest from her expedition from the hospital. She also needed to think. Damien was alive but probably not doing well, based on Murphy's evasiveness. And Brynn Williams was on the run, most likely with Gunner, hiding out of fear.

Murph entered the room, wood floor creaking beneath his feet.

"I need to sleep," she said. "But when I wake, I would like to eat."

He nodded.

"Can you help me out of these sweats? I'm burning up."

"I'll get Margie."

She sat again, unable to stand. Murph left and Margie entered and gently helped her undress.

"I'll bring all that food by later," she said, slipping a sleeveless T-shirt over her head.

"Don't bring it all. I won't be able to eat that much." Kat eased into bed with a groan. "I hate this damn sling." She looked to Margie and managed to smile through her grimace. "Thanks, Margie. For everything."

Murph appeared in the doorway.

"You too, Murph. Thanks."

He made eye contact, and for a moment, she swore she saw him tear up. But when she blinked, the tears were gone and he sighed.

He seemed embarrassed at her gratitude, and she lowered in the bed, Margie lifting the covers over her.

"No need to worry, ya'll. I'm fine."

They smiled. "You're a strong girl," Margie said, joining Murph by the door.

"Everything's locked up tight," Murph said.

"Anything unusual or out of place?"

He thought for a moment. "The basement light was on."

"Really?" It had to be Brynn. She must've come in through the back door. It made sense. Simple doorknob lock, away from prying eyes. She was lucky that Gunner kept most everyone away. She hoped he hadn't caused too much trouble for her.

"Something wrong?" he asked.

She refocused. "No, nothing. I just realized which friend has Gunner. I'll get him in a couple of days. In the meantime," she said, pulling up the covers some more, "you guys can go. I'll be fine."

"You need someone here to—" Murph started.

"I'll have someone," she said quickly. "I've got ya'll, and I'm calling a friend of mine tomorrow. I know she'll come and stay." Of course there was no such person, but she didn't want them to worry, and more than anything, she wanted to be left alone. She could handle things. She always had.

"Fine. But Margie's gonna check on you later when she brings the food."

"Sounds good."

Her eyes grew heavier and they went out of focus.

"What about your bandage?" Margie asked. "Do I need to tend to it?"

"Mm. Bandage?"

"Yes."

Her eyes flickered. "I'm fine, thanks." She could take care of her own bandage. She knew first aid, and she had numerous paramedics as friends if she had questions.

She closed her eyes, and a second or so later, she heard them close the bedroom door. As her body relaxed and her mind began to drift, she knew what she had to do. She had to go after Brynn and bring her in before she got in more trouble. It was the least she could do. After all, she'd risked everything to help her. And then she'd done it again when she'd come after Gunner.

Kat knew she should tell her colleagues, but she also knew that the more of them that showed up, the more likely

Brynn would be to run or to fight it. Bea might even go on the offensive, God only knew with her.

Yes, that's what she would do. And she knew exactly where to go. But first things first. She had to get to Damien.

Her body exhaled, and the world and Brynn Williams drifted away.

CHAPTER FIVE

The cicadas, crickets, and night owls had just silenced as the sun came up on the mountain. Brynn lay very still, window open, dawn filtering in along with the remaining cool night air. She unzipped her sleeping bag and crawled from the old mattress and springs. She'd aired out the mattresses, beaten them with an oar, and sprayed them down with Lysol. Still, she had to cover them with blankets in order to quell the musty smell enough to sleep. Bea, though, hardly seemed to care. She'd gone off in the woods late in the night to no doubt snort her heroin, returning a short while later with a sloppy grin, shuffling like a zombie. She slurred her words and first passed out on the couch, then awoke and collapsed on the front porch, and finally on her bed. Brynn was sick to her stomach over it, and something had to change. She just wasn't sure how.

She rose and crept to Bea's bed to check on her. She was on her side, one arm hanging from the bed, sleeping bag askew. Drool glistened from her cheek, and Brynn made sure she was breathing. Then, satisfied at her coma-like state, Brynn found her bag and searched through it. She found a baggie of pills but no heroin. She looked around the room. Pants. She plucked up her jeans and dug in the pockets. She found three small balloons which she quickly carried from the room. She removed the heavy wood lock on the front door and cringed when the screen door squealed. After closing it carefully, she hurried across the grounds to the woods where she dropped to her knees and dug with her hands. When she was satisfied with the depth of the hole, she dropped in the balloons and buried them, patting the ground flat and covering it with brush. Then she stood and wiped her hands on her jeans.

She walked back to the cabin and considered doing the same with the pills, but she knew Bea would have to have something. Bea would be beyond pissed, but at least she would be alive, rather than passing out in the woods somewhere and getting lost. Or worse, overdosing where it was impossible to get help. At least this way the situation was more controlled.

Gunner whined behind the screen as she stepped up on the porch. The woods smelled thick and rich, and she opened the door to let him out. He jumped on her leg, tail wagging. She scratched his head and they set off for a surveillance walk. They'd been there a few nights, and so far, things had been quiet. She'd parked a ways away and covered the car as best she could to help camouflage it. Gunner hadn't been a problem, barking only when wildlife came up to the house. At night, he kept guard, sleeping by her side, ears perked. But during the day he liked to chase birds and squirrels, and he even went after the crawdads and fish she and Bea caught.

"You like it up here don't you?" He ran up to her with his tongue hanging sideways. He followed her as they climbed for an hour, coming to rest on some high rocks in a clearing. Brynn held out Bea's cell phone and smiled when she got a signal. She dialed the hospital and waited. Hopefully, Vander would be alone this early. A receptionist answered and took a moment to search for her name.

"I'm sorry. It looks like she's no longer a patient here."

Brynn squinted into the rising sun, which was eating the morning mist, infiltrating the trees and ground. "Do you know when she left?"

But the call dropped and she was disconnected. "Your mom's home," Brynn said, causing Gunner to look up at her. Shit, now she had to get him back somehow. But how was more than a good question. According to Uncle Mo, the law was still crawling around like roaches who refused to die. Just when they thought they'd gone, they'd show up again, looking around, asking questions, making threats. Billy was beside himself and was convinced they were following him. She knew he was probably right.

"How long can we do this?" she asked. She sat on a rock and studied the phone. Had Vander told her side of the story yet? What was going on?

She got an idea, but her heart beat too fast to make sense of it. "Should I? Should I call your house?" she asked Gunner. What if it was a setup? What if Vander had told them she had Gunner and they were waiting for her to call? Would Vander do that?

Of course she would. She was a cop.

Brynn stared at the numbers, at the screen with the date and time. She swallowed hard and dialed, too curious to know how she was, if she was okay, consequences be damned. She had to know and she didn't know why. She had no ties to Vander or any cop for that matter. So why did she care so much? Was it human decency or something more?

She dialed information and asked for Vander's home number. There was no listing.

She ended the call and then dialed Holly, hoping for information. Holly answered on the third ring.

"Brynn."

"Yeah. How are things going? They on to you yet?" Holly had lent her the car. It had been her father's, and he was in a personal care home, so he wouldn't miss it.

"All is quiet with me. But ya'll are all over the news."

"Still?"

"Yes."

"What about Vander? Any word on her?"

"She's home."

"Is she—okay?"

Holly paused. "I guess. Why?"

"I'm just wondering why she hasn't cleared us yet. Or at least made it safe enough for us to come in."

"I don't know. I just know her partner is still critical. I think she's been sticking by him. There's footage of her leaving his hospital and she doesn't look so good herself."

Brynn ran her hand through her hair. She was dirty and dying for a shower. As it was, they were bathing in the creek. Cold mountain water was great for some things, but early in the morning, you didn't want to soak in it.

"I don't know what to do," Brynn said. "Bea's a mess."

"Come here."

"We can't. You know that." She wasn't surprised that Holly had asked. Holly was a good friend but a bit clingy, even after their dating had ended. She still wanted something more and she made it more than obvious. It probably hadn't been a good idea to go to her for help, but Brynn hadn't had much of a choice.

"I'll call soon," Brynn said and ended the call as Holly was replying, asking her again to come home. She climbed down the rocks and whistled for Gunner, who followed happily. They walked the near hour back to the cabin and saw no one and no recent tire prints. Brynn relaxed a little and stopped at the creek where she stripped and waded in, the cold water taking her breath. She walked to just above her knees and splashed the water up on her arms, shoulders, and face. Then she sat, bent back, and dunked her head. When she came up, she shouted from the cold running down her back and opened her eyes to Gunner barking, crossing the creek himself. She watched him climb out and run playfully. Then, as if a switch had been flipped, he stopped, ears pointed, and barked back across the creek. Quickly, she stood and looked around, hurrying from the water.

"What is it? Who's there?"

Someone stepped out from behind a tree, and Brynn screamed and knelt for a heavy rock. She charged and was about to throw it when the figure stepped out of the shade and into the sunlight.

Vander held up her hand, her other arm in a sling. She was thinner and pale but with red coloring her high cheekbones. Brynn stared her down, rock in hand, chest heaving with panic.

She looked around and felt like prey surrounded by predators. "You alone?" Brynn asked.

Vander nodded and shifted her gaze after sweeping up and down Brynn's nude body.

Brynn dropped the rock and pointed a finger at her.

"You scared the absolute shit out of me."

"I'm sorry. I didn't know how else to approach." She continued to look away. She had a backpack slung over her good shoulder, and she was dressed in cargo shorts, a light T-shirt, and hiking boots. By the look of the dirt caking her socks, it looked like she'd been walking awhile.

Brynn honed in on a stain, a dark red plume above her sling near her shoulder.

"You're bleeding."

Vander shifted and gave her a quick glance. "I know."

"Bullet wound?" Brynn turned and found her clothes, then scrambled to pull them on over her wet skin. She could feel her own face reddening from the exposure, and Vander's reaction hadn't helped. Why was she so afraid to look anywhere near her?

"Yes. I think I need to change the dressing."

From across the creek, Gunner barked and rushed into the water, swimming across and scrambling for footing in the mud. He rushed Vander and jumped on her, nearly knocking her down.

Vander laughed, stumbling backward. "Whoa, boy." She knelt and showered him with as much affection as she could with one hand. Gunner returned the love, licking her face and neck, whining with excitement. Vander continued laughing, now kissing him on his snout and hugging his neck. "I can't believe how much I've missed this guy," she said.

Brynn tugged on her shirt, very much aware that the cotton material was sticking to her breasts. She plucked it a few times trying to get some air in there, but it was no use. Instead she ran fingers through her wet hair. "He's been great. A really good dog." She wiped her hands on her pants and Vander stood, looking weak. She leaned on a walking stick.

"Are you okay?" Brynn asked. "You don't look so good."

Vander wiped her brow with a bandana, then slipped it back into her pocket. "Thanks for taking care of him," she said, a little short of breath. She took a few steps and then looked like she was going to go down. Brynn rushed to her side, steadying her.

"You're far from okay." She turned her and led her toward the cabin. This Vander was far from the one she'd always seen around town. The Vander she was used to was tall, strong, confident, and walked like she could kick some serious ass. The cop walk. This Vander was pale, trembling, and about to pass out. "You shouldn't be up here," Brynn said. "Especially not on your own."

"Yeah, well, my friends wouldn't exactly want to approach you in a friendly manner."

Brynn led her up the steps and the old boards creaked. "Probably not," she said. "They think we're involved don't they? With those guys that shot at you."

"They have questions, yes."

Brynn opened the screen door and they entered quietly. She eased Vander onto the couch and then went to the kitchen and dug in the cooler for a bottled water. She twisted it open and gave it to Vander who thanked her and drank heartily. She set the bottle down and wiped her mouth with the back of her hand.

"I didn't realize how thirsty I was." But she still trembled, and despite trying to smile and hide her shaking hand, Brynn saw.

"One of two things need to happen here. One, you take off your gear, lie back, and let me help, or two, we get to your car and I drive you back to town and get you some help. For number two to happen you need to promise me some sort of protection. I don't want to go back to prison."

"I can't promise you anything. You know that."

"So I have to hide forever?"

Vander shook her head. "Just come in and talk. I've told them my side. Told them you saved me. The rest…be honest. Tell them what happened." She paused and eased the pack off her shoulder with a wince. "Bea isn't involved is she? With those guys?"

Brynn felt anger rise. "No, of course not. She was just picking me up from prison. I mean I literally had just been released. Your high-speed chase got in our way. And when I saw what was happening, what was I supposed to do? Turn around and drive off? Leave you for dead?"

Vander licked dry lips. "Most are surprised you didn't."

"Yeah, well, most don't know shit about me and who I really am. They just hear I'm a Williams and assume the worst."

Vander looked around, and Brynn could see her eyes growing heavy. "Bea?"

Brynn motioned toward the bedroom. "Asleep."

"She okay with coming in if I bring you in?"

Brynn was honest. "I doubt it."

"Will you?"

Brynn sighed and paced the floor. Their hiding spot was useless now. Vander would tell; she would have to. Bea…she didn't know what to do about Bea. But as far as herself, she was tired of running. Tired of looking over her shoulder. This was not freedom. And freedom, pure freedom, was what she wanted most.

"Promise me something and I will," Brynn said.

Vander stared deep into her eyes. "If I can."

"Let me drive. And let me get you some help."

Vander laughed a little. "That's it? You're worried about me?"

"Yes."

"Why, Williams? I'm just a cop. The one who put you away."

Brynn stared at her in disbelief, surprised at her words. "I—I care. I saved your ass didn't I? Why would I let you die now?"

"Oh, so it's pride." She grinned and Brynn felt her heart jerk with a start. Then it fluttered.

"Maybe."

"In that case, yes, I promise. You can drive and you can get me some help. And…a little advice from me to you. Ask for an attorney."

"Oh, I plan on it."

Vander gave a nod. "Good."

She struggled to stand and Brynn helped. From the bedroom they heard a long groan as if someone was waking and stretching. Brynn tried to cut Bea off at the doorway, but it was too late. She was standing there, eyes wide, staring at Vander.

"What the fuck?" She looked around wildly, then hurried to the window to peek outside. "Where are they? Are we surrounded?"

"Bea." Brynn tried to grab her, but she pulled away, hurrying back to the bedroom to slip on her jeans and step into her shoes. "Bea, we're fine. We're safe. It's just her."

"Just her my ass. They're out there. I can smell them." She didn't bother to tie her laces.

Vander spoke, and her tone surprised Brynn, though she'd heard it many times before while in town and when she and Bea had first been pulled over four years ago.

"Williams, sit down. We need to talk."

Bea froze, pushed her shoulders back, and turned to look at Vander.

"You expect me to listen to you? Cop?"

"I do and you will. If you want information that is."

Bea, head held high, scoffed but walked to the chair and sat down. Vander sat as well. Brynn watched, nerves on edge.

"I came alone," Vander said. "I had a hunch about this cabin. Had heard the story about Jasper being your true grandfather. I told no one. I knew you would run or there would be a standoff if my colleagues came. And that would most likely get you in more trouble and I know you didn't want it. Especially since you were kind enough to see to Gunner. I figured you wanted peace, wanted this whole thing over. That's why I'm here."

"It's about time," Bea said. "Fucking hell, do you know what we've been through in trying to hide? The whole county wants our heads on a platter."

Vander held up her hand. "I've been shot. Five times. One hit my shoulder. I nearly died from blood loss. My partner... he's critical. We don't know if he's going to wake up, and if he does, who he's going to be." Her voice faltered as she spoke of him. "He's...he just lies there, machine breathing for him, machines beeping around him." She paused and swallowed. "He was hit in the shoulder, arm, and head. It's a miracle he's alive."

Bea started to speak, but Brynn gave her shoulder a squeeze to stop her.

"Thanks to you we're alive." She closed her eyes. "I'm alive. And I want to bring you in, tell them the truth once again. That you came upon the scene in innocence and protected my partner and me at your own behest. Because you knew it was the right thing to do."

"Whole lot a good that did us," Bea said.

"I suppose you think now that our lives weren't worth the trouble?"

Bea mumbled something and Brynn smacked her arm.

"Well, like it or not you need to come with me back into town and give a statement. I've already told your sister that I'll do what I can and stand in your corner. But I've also advised her to get a lawyer. I can only protect you so much, and I can't bend or change the law."

Bea stood, hands in fists. "Forget it then. If all we get is your half-assed attempt at a good word for us, then fuck that. I'll take my chances on my own."

"Bea, don't," Brynn said. "Don't do this."

"No, Brynn. Fuck her. We save her life and this is what we get?"

"She's offering us her very best. She came to get us on her own, to make it better for us. Can't you see how she's helping?"

Bea stared Vander down. "And if her partner dies, or ends up with a brain like a marshmallow…then what? What will she do then? Who will save us?"

Vander took a step forward, anger marking her cheeks and neck. "Don't talk about Damien that way."

Bea stared back. "Or what? You gonna beat me with one arm?"

Vander took another step. "I'll take you down and arrest you with one arm."

Bea laughed. "Bullshit. You're about to keel over." She headed for the bedroom and again yanked her arm away from Brynn who tried to stop her.

"Bea, don't."

"You can go in with her," Bea said. "But there ain't no way I'm trusting her or them."

Brynn gave Vander a pleading look. "Can't you do something, say something?"

Vander closed her eyes. "I've said all I can. I don't want to make promises I can't keep."

Brynn cursed and went to the bedroom. Bea was shoving her things into her duffel.

"I'm going. Gonna take the car. Try to give me as much of a head start as you can."

"Bea, please don't."

"I don't have a choice, Brynn. They'll lock me up. This time for years. You know my rap sheet. Then there's the stolen car, the guns. I'm fucked. No matter what your sweet cop says."

"My sweet cop? What the hell is that supposed to mean?"

Bea laughed. "You're sweet on her."

Brynn tightened her fists and felt her nails almost penetrate her palms. "I am not."

"Yes, you are. Just like when you were thirteen and you had that thing for Ms. Albright. You think I don't know, don't notice, but you're wrong. You're just a dyke. Simple as that. And now you've fallen for a dyke cop. And I need to get the hell out of here."

She hurriedly dug in her pockets and panic came over her face. She dug everything back out of her bag.

"What the fuck, what the fuck..." She was desperate, searching for her smack.

"Your heroin is gone," Brynn said. "Save yourself the trouble."

Bea straightened slowly and turned, the look of the devil on her face and burning red beneath her skin.

"What did you say?"

Brynn walked from the room, unwilling to fight. She was already pissed enough that Bea wouldn't give in and come in to give a statement. They couldn't run forever. And her comment about being sweet on Vander had embarrassed her. She hoped Vander hadn't heard. Dyke? Is that really how Bea wanted to leave things? If Vander wasn't there, it was very likely that she'd get into a fierce wrestling match with her younger sister over such words. There was disrespect and ignoring her advice and rules, but this...this was unacceptable. Who she was and who she was drawn to was no one's business, and she'd tried to keep it that way the majority of her life. She'd even dated a few boys in high school for good measure.

"Everything okay?" Vander asked, turning from the living room window to face her. She appeared concerned, and Brynn searched for any kind of tick or blush that showed embarrassment. She saw nothing. Only the pale, gaunt face of an injured woman.

"We should go," Brynn said. She grabbed her jacket, her duffel bag, and baseball cap. There was no sense in staying, and Vander was looking really bad.

"She's not coming," Vander said.

"No."

"I'll have to tell them where she is."

"I know."

"I'm sorry about that."

"I understand." Brynn opened the door and Vander whistled for Gunner who bolted out before them. Brynn waited by the door for Vander to exit, but Vander seemed to want to be the polite one. She waved Brynn through and followed her out. They both squinted in the morning sun.

"Where's your car?" Brynn asked. "I can go get it."

Vander stepped off the porch steps and walked ahead. "It's this way."

Brynn watched in disbelief for a moment but then caught up with her, walking back into the woods. Brynn wanted to ask her questions, but Vander was breathing hard and sweating. They walked through thick brush with Gunner crashing through ahead of them. Brynn noticed that Vander had come through the back, behind the cabin. Her car, a black Chevy crossover, was through the brush where it couldn't be seen or heard. Brynn had a feeling Vander had been more than careful, had watched for a while.

"How long have you been here?"

They paused at the car and Vander dug the keys out and unlocked the doors. Hesitantly, she handed the keys over to Brynn.

"Since yesterday evening. I had to make sure you were alone and had no guns."

"How could you possibly know that?"

"I snuck in when you two went to the creek." She waved Brynn off as Brynn tried to walk with her to the passenger door.

"Why didn't you say something then?"

Vander opened the door slowly and tried to hide a wince. "I was hoping to get you alone."

Brynn thought back to the creek. How she had stripped and bathed nude, not a care in the world. How long had Vander been watching? She couldn't help but ask; she had to know.

"Why didn't you talk to me before I stripped and got in the creek?"

Vander flushed and slid in the car, shut the door, and looked straight ahead. Brynn climbed in next to her, watching her intently. Vander's jaw flexed as if she were thinking deeply or nervous or both. The sight caused a stirring in Brynn's chest.

"I had to make sure you wouldn't run," Vander said. She lowered her gaze but still didn't look at Brynn. Then she struggled with her seat belt. Brynn reached to help, but Vander snapped.

"I'm fine. Really."

Brynn paused, almost afraid to move. She backed away, studied her for a moment, and then started the car. An apology obviously wasn't coming, but she brushed it off, knowing Vander felt like hell.

The plume of blood on the shoulder had spread. "I should really take a look at that before we get going. Stop the bleeding."

Vander closed her eyes as if she were fighting pain or impatience. "No. Just drive."

Brynn, losing patience herself, put the car in gear. "Where to?"

"The station."

Brynn gunned the engine. There was no way in hell they were going to the station. The first stop was going to be the hospital. How could her family and friends let her go off on her own? And hadn't anyone tended to her wound? Brynn thought cops stuck together, looked out for one another. It didn't make sense.

Brynn drove through the thick brush and found the trail. They bumped and swayed, but she didn't slow. Brynn eyed Gunner in the back who sat watching the road, tongue hanging from his mouth.

"You did all this for us didn't you?" Brynn asked. "You kept it secret so you could come on your own."

Vander leaned against the door, eyes closed. "Had to. Saved me. Kept Gunner safe."

Brynn glanced at her. Her eyes didn't open again, and her breathing changed as her tense body fell limp. After checking her wrist for a pulse, Brynn sat back and drove, destination hospital, future unknown.

CHAPTER SIX

"Vander. Vander?" Kat felt her heavy eyes flutter open. The room was bright, harsh. She brought her arm up to shade her sensitive vision, but she found it difficult. A cord of some sort was connected to her hand.

"Easy," a familiar voice said. She felt a warm hand cover hers.

"Murph?"

"In the flesh."

She turned her head and found him smiling beneath the bill of a worn camouflage Tarheel hat. His shirt matched his hat in different shades of green, but his pants were thick denim, mud smeared on one knee. He wasn't wearing his firearm.

She couldn't yet make sense of any of it. "Where—"

"You're in the emergency room."

"What?" She tried to sit up, but he eased her down. She closed her eyes in frustration, and suddenly, the noise all around her penetrated. A baby crying, beeps, coughs, loud orders, soft, soothing talk. She lifted her tethered hand and found an IV. "Why?"

He sat slowly, carefully, as if she'd fly out of the bed at any moment. "Your wound was bleeding and infected. And you were very weak. You're lucky you got here when you did."

"Brynn?" She stared directly into his brown eyes. His face fell in a microsecond and then recovered, but she had seen it; it was too late. "Where, Murph?"

"We took her in."

"She brought me here and you took her in? Did you arrest her?"

He looked down and stared at his hands. "We had no choice. Had no answers. And you, you had disappeared, and then she shows with you near death and covered in dirt. What were we supposed to do?"

She tensed, but it caused pain up in her shoulder. She was still in a sling. "Damn it, get this thing off me."

Again, Murph stood and eased her busy hands. He did so firmly yet gently. He shushed her quietly as if soothing a fussy babe. "You have to relax and be still. That antibiotic needs to get into your body."

She jerked away from him, so frustrated she could scream. It caused a huge stab of pain to course through her, but she didn't care. Her anger was winning out. "Can't they give me a shot? Two shots? I need to get to Brynn."

"So you're on a first-name basis with her now?"

Her mind raced right over his question. First, the cabin, Brynn's nude body, the argument with Bea and then the drive ho—"Fucking shit, where's Gunner? He's not in the car is he?"

Murph shook his head and tried to grip her hand. "Williams said you two dropped him off at your house."

Kat leaned back and took a big breath. She could remember nothing after leaving the cabin. Brynn could've taken her anywhere, done anything. But once again, she'd brought her to where she needed to be. Even if it wasn't what she currently wanted.

Murph tugged on the bill of his cap and rubbed his stubble. He still had a baby face no matter how hard he tried to hide it.

"You been fishing?" she asked. He was dirty, black under his nails and in his nail beds. He'd been digging for worms.

"Yeah."

"They called you in?"

"We were all worried sick when you disappeared, Vander. Captain Bowman insisted I take the day off instead of pacing the floors looking for you."

"I had something I had to do."

"Like go get the Williams girl. You know how much shit you're in?"

Kat looked away. "She hasn't done anything wrong."

He rested his elbows on his knees and stared at the floor. "I hope you're right."

"I am. Now when can I get out of here?"

The curtain scraped as a woman entered wearing creased khakis, a maroon button-up blouse, and a lab coat. She carried a metal clipboard and a stern look. "Kat Vander, I presume?"

Kat didn't speak, just squared off with her with her steady, steely gaze.

"You're either very stubborn or very brave," she said. "I can't decide which one. Luckily, it's not my job to figure you out. It's my job to fix you up."

"When can I go?" Kat asked, in no mood for lectures.

The woman laughed and set down the clipboard. She placed her hands in her pockets and looked to Murph.

"I'm going to go with stubborn," she said.

Murph laughed. "You have no idea."

"Hello, I can hear you. I'm sitting right here."

The woman, whose name was Dr. Sands according to her lab coat, took a hand out of her pocket to rest it on Kat's.

"I'm sorry. It's just that you had quite a worried crowd here and they've all filled me in on your…"

"Stubbornness."

"Yes."

"Great." Kat glared at Murph who reddened. "Now when can I leave?"

Sands squeezed her hand. "We cleaned out your wound. Re-bandaged. And now we're giving you a strong antibiotic."

"And…"

"And you can go home when it's finished. But only if you promise to stay on bed rest for the next few days. And if that wound gets worse in any way, your behind better get back in here pronto."

"I'm good with that," Kat said.

"But I have to admit, I have my doubts about you being able to do that, Ms. Vander. Based on your recent behavior and that stubbornness your fellow officers have told me about, I'm going out on a limb here and trusting you."

"I can do it." She looked to Murph and gave him a look that caused him to straighten and speak.

"I can see that she does."

Dr. Sands raised an eyebrow. "An infection like this is very serious. You understand that don't you?"

Kat nodded and resisted rolling her eyes.

Dr. Sands patted her hand. "Very well. I'll start your discharge papers and get you a script for more antibiotics. You have to take them twice a day. Understood?"

"Yes."

Dr. Sands looked at Murph. "Keep a close eye on her the next week or so."

"You got it."

Kat groaned. She hated being treated like a child. She could take care of herself. She didn't need Murph and Margie in her home, jumping every time she stumbled or sneezed. She had Gunner and a phone, and that was all she needed.

Dr. Sands left the curtained room and Kat turned on Murph. "I don't need you up my ass twenty-four seven. Got it?"

Murph smiled. "Doctor's orders."

"Fucking shit, Murph, I'm fine. Tell everyone I'm fine."

"But you're not."

"Murph. Hooker. Diamond." The words sank in slowly. She could almost see them penetrate.

He yanked off his hat and rubbed his hair in frustration. "She won't believe it, Vander. I haven't done anything wrong." He shook his head. "I'll call your bluff, Vander. I will."

Kat smiled. "No, you won't."

He stood and smacked his cap against his thigh. "Mother fuck, Vander."

He was cursing. This was a good sign. She had gotten to him. He was putty in her hands now. "You know they say that even the thought of cheating can be considered cheating."

"Enough. Just stop. You win."

"Great. Thanks, Murph. Now, I believe that IV is empty. Help me get dressed and get the hell out of here."

❖

"Vander, we shouldn't be here," Murph said, desperation high in his voice. He scrambled after her and opened the door to the station for her.

"I have to make things right," she said. "I know you know what I mean, Murph." She looked him in the eye. "We do what's right, don't we? Brynn is innocent. She saved my life and Damien's. Then she even went and got Gunner to care for him. Why? Because I asked her to. Now what do you call that, Murph? A crime?"

She entered the station when Murph didn't respond and walked straight ahead and eyed Johnnie Madison on the right behind the counter.

"Christ on a cracker," he said when he saw her. "Vander, you okay?" He brushed crumbs off his broad chest and stared at her. He began swatting George Marks who was sitting and typing at the computer. Mads and Marks. It was damn good to see them.

"I'm well, Mads, thanks for asking." She stopped at the locked door. Marks looked up and his face went ashen. He stood at attention. "Ma'am," he said. "Welcome back."

"She's not back," Murph said.

"Not yet," she corrected him.

Madison buzzed her in, and they walked into the inner workings of her police station.

Phones rang, the strong smell of coffee permeated the air. The gray industrial carpet was worn into a trail, leading the way to each section. When they came to homicide, she smelled microwave popcorn and found the detectives at their desks, heads in files and computers. When she came to her captain's desk, he was busy thumbing through papers and talking softly to another colleague, Lenny Tanner. When they sensed a presence, they looked up then did a double take. Captain Bowman stood.

"Vander, what in the hell are you doing here?"

But she was busy looking around, walking to look in on the interrogation room. "Where is she? Where's Brynn Williams?"

"She's in holding, why?"

"You got her locked up?"

He nodded. "For the time being, yes."

"Get her out. Get her in here."

Captain Bowman looked to Murph who threw up his hands. Tanner moved quickly and pulled up a chair for Kat, and she knew she must still look like death warmed over with her pale pallor and dirt coated hiking clothes. Her shirt had a big bloodstain on it.

"Sit, sit," Tanner said, easing her down.

"I'm okay. Really. Thanks."

"Cap, I need to clear some things up," she said. "Brynn Williams has done nothing wrong. You can't lock her up."

He cleared his throat and leaned against the front of his desk, hefty arms crossed.

"Vander, you're in no condition to be discussing this right now. You need to be home—"

"No. I'm giving a statement. Now."

He rubbed his forehead.

"The sooner I get it out, the sooner I can get home."

His eyebrows rose, as if confirming she might be right. He looked to Tanner. "Get the recorder, the camera." He stared at Kat. "I hope you know what you're doing."

"I do."

"This is just a statement. You know there will be an investigation and most likely a hearing."

"I'm well aware."

He looked to the ceiling and sighed. "All right, Vander. We're all ears."

Tanner set up the equipment in the interrogation room, and the four of them entered with Murph sitting next to her. He squeezed her good shoulder for support.

Captain Bowman started, and she relayed her name and badge number. They discussed the incident, which Captain Bowman knew something about based on her earlier comments. She confirmed what she said before, about Brynn and Bea coming on the scene in innocence and helping. She reaffirmed that they had saved her life, along with Damien's, by reporting the situation.

"Why did they run?" Captain Bowman asked. "Why didn't they stay?"

"Brynn did stay. She stayed by my side until they took me away for surgery. And she said she left because she knew the car they had been in was stolen, and she was worried about the guns. She had literally just stepped out of prison. She didn't want to go back."

Captain Bowman again cleared his throat and crossed thick fingers as his arms rested on the table.

"See, that's the problem, Vander. The vehicle they were in was stolen. And as for the guns, we're not sure because we can't locate them. But word on the street is Bea bought them off Robbie Kinnison, so we can bet they were stolen. We can't erase these infractions because they helped you."

Kat licked her lips and nodded. "I know, Cap. But what if I told you it was solely Bea who stole the car and bought the guns? Brynn was just a bystander. She was in prison a mere thirty minutes before the shootout. Bea picked her up in the stolen car and had the weapons already in there. Brynn is innocent. Her only crime is her fear of us assuming and jumping to conclusions because of her name and returning her to prison."

Captain Bowman again rubbed his forehead. "We need to know how and why you went after them without us." His voice shook, and she knew the questions had been bothering him. Captain Bowman had been like a father to her, and she felt a wave of guilt smack her in the face. She was the goody-goody—no errors, no infractions, no complaints. She was the exemplary officer. Now she had done something questionable and it wasn't sitting well with him.

"I, uh, had a hunch as to where they were hiding." She tried to hold their gazes, but they wouldn't hold hers. "Years ago, I heard a rumor from a dying Grace Williams. I was called to the house because Bea feared she was already dead. She was just about eight at the time. I walked in the room, saw her state, and called EMS. I then sat next to her and held her hand. She was dying, emphysema, COPD. She was mumbling to me. Said Jasper was her daddy."

"Jasper Cole?" Captain Bowman asked.

"Yes, sir. She kept repeating it. And then…she just gasped a few times about a minute apart, and then she didn't gasp anymore. She died."

They were silent for a moment before Kat continued. "Anyway, I always kept that with me. And I had known Jasper as a child and knew he had a cabin up by Whistler's Creek in the Spruceville Mountains. So when the Williams girls went missing, I figured they might go there. Not many people knew of it, and no one knew that Jasper was their blood."

"So I went up alone to check it out. I knew if I had told you, you would've sent out the Calvary, and Bea might have shot and put them in more trouble than they were already in."

"Speaking of Bea," Captain Bowman said. "Where is she?"

"Last I saw of her she was at the cabin. But she refused to come with me, and I was too weak to subdue her. I do know she's hard up for heroin. She most likely will venture back into town to score."

Murph stood. "I'll send some patrol up to the cabin and get a current APB on Bea." He left the room.

Captain Bowman rubbed his chin. "Brynn gonna back up your story?"

Kat scoffed a little. "Don't be surprised if she refuses to incriminate Bea. She's apparently spent her lifetime covering for her."

He nodded. He looked to Tanner who turned off the camera.

"She really save your life?" he asked.

"Yes, sir. Held me in her arms in the backseat. Held pressure on my wound."

He stood. "Okay. We'll take it from here."

Kat stood and they exited the room. She took a deep breath and felt the world crumble from her shoulders. "Can we get her now?"

Captain Bowman sunk into his chair behind his cluttered desk. "You know better than that, Vander. She has to give a statement. And you can't be here."

Murph returned and gently cupped her elbow. "Let's get you home."

Kat wanted to stand and argue. To insist they release Brynn then and now. But she knew Captain Bowman was right, and Murph was so gentle yet strong right next to her. She leaned into him and nodded, the stress of the day finally catching up to her.

"Okay, let's go."

CHAPTER SEVEN

B rynn didn't bother to rise from the table when the officers did. Instead she sat and rubbed her sore wrists and sipped her now warm Coke. They'd questioned her for an hour, and honestly, she was surprised it hadn't been for longer. They'd asked specific questions, mostly aimed at her knowledge of the stolen vehicle and weapons. It was obvious they'd already spoken to someone about the incident. One question had surprised her. They'd wanted to know why she'd helped. Why she'd held pressure on Vander's wound. How she knew what to do. After the surprise of the questions, she'd found herself offended. They really must think her completely heartless and apathetic. That's what a name will get you.

It hadn't always been like this. Her grandparents had been good people, hard working, respected. They'd purchased the acres of land that the family now lived on, known as Williams Lane. But things had gone to hell with her parents. Both had died early, her father suddenly. It had sucked the life out of everyone. Taken the wind from their sails. And it had forced her into a motherly role.

The door clicked open, and the man she knew as the captain walked in with another officer. They didn't bother to sit.

"We just got off the phone with corrections. It seems you did quite well for yourself inside."

"I tried to, sir."

"They had nothing but good things to say. And they confirmed the time of your release."

She waited for more. Finally, the captain spoke. "Ms. Williams, we just have one more question for you before you're free to go."

She sat back, hands in her lap. It sounded like they were letting her go. No prison. She couldn't believe it. She began to tremble again and stuck her hands between her knees to hide it.

"We need to know where Bea is."

She stared at the captain, unblinking. "I honestly have no idea."

He gave an eat shit and die grin, and this time he sat. His large, hard as a boulder body creaked and groaned as he shifted for comfort. He sighed and rubbed a temple where the gray in his hair was the most prominent. He was in bad need of a trim around the ears. She guessed he had been putting in a lot of overtime since the shooting. Tired eyes and a grim set to his mouth seemed to confirm her theory.

"You don't expect us to believe that do you?"

She shook her head in defiance. "I don't care if you do or not. I have no idea where she's going. All I can tell you is I buried her heroin, left her some pills, and left her at the cabin. She said she was leaving but didn't say where."

"But had she said, you wouldn't tell us would you?"

Her hands grew more restless and her knees bobbed up and down. "I don't know."

The captain planted his palms on the table. "That's what I thought."

"Look, you can follow me, bug my house, my phone. You'll see I don't know."

"Oh, we've done that. And will continue to do so. Because whether you like it or not, Bea will be held responsible for these charges."

Blood drained from her face. "Which charges?"

"The stolen vehicle. Leaving the scene of a crime. We can't prove the weapons charge until we find them. Resisting arrest. And I'm sure there will be more to add to that as time goes on."

"Why am I not being charged?"

"Do you want to be?"

She looked away and chewed her lower lip. "No, sir."

"Then count your blessings." He stood with more groans and creaks. "One more thing." He stuck out his hand. "Thank you for saving my people. They wouldn't be alive without you."

She reached up and took his powerful hand. He squeezed and she did too. She went limp to release, but he held firm.

"Stay out of trouble, Williams."

She nodded once. "Yes, sir."

"And if you hear from your sister, you better call in. You can't protect her this time. And just so you know, I will charge you with harboring a fugitive."

He released her hand and motioned for the other officer to open the door. They filed out and the officer held the door for her. She exited with her Coke and stood, unsure what to do.

The officer touched her shoulder. "You're free to go."

She nodded and acted as if she knew that. She walked through the station feeling completely out of place, like a long tailed cat in a room full of rocking chairs. Curious eyes from different people in different departments stared her down. No doubt they'd seen her face and kept their eye out for her and Bea the past couple of days.

Would she ever find peace in this town? She was beginning to doubt it. Her name, it seemed, would always be a tattoo on her forehead screaming trouble. She stepped through the main doors and breathed in the heavy humid air.

She needed a ride home and a bath. She couldn't call Holly…Bea still had her car. No doubt she would get an earful for that. But she knew Bea would ditch it soon if she hadn't already. Brynn shoved her hands in her pockets and walked to the road. Tired as she was, she began the walk home, staying off in the grassy shoulder, head low. She recalled that some of her belongings were still in Vander's car, unless she'd dropped them off, which she doubted, considering her condition. And even though she knew she could get by without them, something drew her to go after them.

She kept on down the road, then turned, sighed, and walked backward. She stuck out her thumb and eyed each car as it drove by. The good thing was, she knew a hell of a lot of people in this county. And the bad news was she knew a hell of a lot of people in this county. Thanks to Bea and Billy, the churchgoing folks steered clear, and those that didn't had respect for her grandparents. After about ten cars, an old truck slowed and pulled over. She hustled to the door and pulled it open. Clyde Beaufort gave her a nod and she crawled in, already smelling his dip. As if on cue, he picked up the tin can from between his legs and spit.

"Whatcha doin' out here, Brynn Williams?"

"I was at the station," she said, searching for an absent seat belt. She rolled down her window and rested her arm on the frame.

Clyde had been a family friend for ages. He had known her grandparents and had to be in his eighties himself. He eased back on the road and drove slowly, cars passing him by. She studied his worn overalls, dirty white T-shirt, and dirty hands. His small head was covered with a straw fedora.

"Been in the garden today?" Brynn asked.

"Yep. Got beans that need stringin' and snappin'."

"I bet you do."

"Pickling some beets too. Ya'll want some?"

"Yes, sir." She smiled. His tasted just like her grandfather's.

"Am I taking you home?"

"Well, sir, I need to go down to the lake first. My belongings are down there with a friend." She didn't give details, and she knew he wouldn't ask. He was more like her grandfather, a man of few words.

He picked up his can and spit again. "I can take you there."

"I'd really appreciate it."

"I'll do it for some of your canned pickles."

He looked over at her and smiled. She nodded. "Deal."

They drove on in silence, and Brynn hoped Vander was home by now and not still in the hospital. If she was still in the hospital, Brynn would check on Gunner. If not, she'd get her belongings, check on Vander, and get a ride back. God, she couldn't wait for that bath. Sweat and creek water were stuck to her skin, and her hair was plastered to her head. She was sure she looked a sight.

When they reached the turnoff, Brynn gave Clyde directions. He drove slowly through the neighborhood streets until they reached Vander's house. She reached over, gave him a kiss on the cheek, and crossed to Vander's front door where she rang the doorbell. Her vehicle was in the driveway, and the sun was just setting on the lake.

Brynn bobbed on the balls of her feet, nervous and a little surprised at it. She wiped suddenly sweaty palms on her stiff jeans. Shouting came from inside, along with barking.

The door opened.

"Damn it, Murph, I'm fine—" Vander's face peeked out, and she stopped speaking when she saw Brynn.

"Hi." Brynn gave a little wave and then felt stupid and hid her hand behind her back. Beyond her, Clyde drove off, waving to them both.

"Was that Clyde Beaufort?" Vander asked.

"He, uh, gave me a lift."

"Yeah, he's good like that." Vander opened her door a little farther and Gunner snuck out to assault Brynn with excited kisses. Brynn knelt and loved him back. She looked up when Vander didn't speak. They locked eyes, and something unspoken passed between them. Brynn felt it, and by the blush on Vander's pale cheeks, she knew she felt it too.

"I just came for my belongings," Brynn said, breaking the silence.

Vander backed away and pushed open the door. "Oh, of course." She laughed and it sounded nervous.

Brynn stepped inside, noticed the smell of hot apple pie, and glanced around. The house was decorated in antique country. Whitewashed wood floors, weathered white cabinets, and expensive looking furniture. And it smelled wonderful, like a warm night on the beach.

"Nice house," she said, continuing to notice things like the bookcases, the fireplace, the throw pillows, and matching curtains. It was very charming, cozy. It was the perfect home for being on the water. Light, airy.

Vander crossed the kitchen and made her way to the door leading to the driveway. Brynn's bag was there, waiting.

"I shoulda had Murph drop it off," Vander said. "Sorry."

"No, it's fine. Really."

Vander didn't pick it up, and Brynn noticed her tired eyes and limp body. A piece of pie was half eaten on a plate at the table.

"I'm sorry. I interrupted your pie." The rest of the pie sat steaming in the center.

Vander waved her off. "Oh, it's just Murph's doing. His wife, Margie, is quite the master in the kitchen. That thing probably has two sticks of butter in it."

Brynn laughed. "Anything Southern does. That's what makes it good."

"Is that what it is?"

Brynn laughed. "Of course."

Vander pointed a finger at her. "What about fried? You know how much fried chicken I have in my fridge right now? It's insane. And the rest of it Murph has. He and Margie tried their best to stuff me while they've been here, as you can see." She eyed the pie, then lifted her plate and deposited it in the sink. Gunner followed, licking his lips.

"Would you like some?" Vander asked, turning from the sink. "I've got potato salad, slaw, green beans, pintos, macaroni and cheese—" She stopped. "God, you name it, I've pretty much got it."

Brynn smiled. "I really shouldn't. I need to get home and clean up."

Vander nodded and looked off in the distance. "But you don't have a ride do you?"

"Oh, don't worry about that. I hitched here. I can hitch back."

Vander's eyes widened in what looked like disbelief. "You hitchhike?"

Brynn shrugged. "Sure."

Vander grabbed her forehead. "Don't you know how dangerous that is?"

Brynn laughed again. "Here? Never. I know everyone."

"No, you don't. Trust me on that. And a beautiful woman like you…no way you should be doing that."

Brynn looked away and felt herself blushing. Vander too, averted her gaze and swallowed. She swayed a little, and Brynn rushed to her side. "What can I do? Where do you need to go?"

"The bathroom."

"'K. Tell me where to go and I'll help you." They began to walk, and Brynn felt Vander start to pull away, but she seemed to change her mind and leaned into her. Her strong body was firm and warm. Brynn could feel her muscles move in her lower back and forearm. It stirred her and she realized she was feeling desire, something she hadn't felt in a long while.

"You mean you don't know?"

"No, should I?"

"Didn't you come in my house? When you got Gunner?"

"No, of course not. That would be really…weird. He came into the basement to me. I took him from there."

"Oh, and here I thought you thoroughly snooped."

"And swiped a few things while I was at it?"

Vander didn't answer. She pointed down the hallway from the living room, and Brynn helped her along. But Vander's assumptions about her stung, and she felt compelled to correct her, to stand up for herself.

"I'm not my sister, you know. Or Billy, though I really think he just does what Bea tells him to do."

Vander spoke softly. "I'm beginning to see that."

"Beginning to? Geez, what else do I have to do?"

Vander laughed. "Swear in blood on the Bible."

"Swear what? That I'm a good girl? I wouldn't go that far."

"No?"

They stopped at the bathroom door and faced one another. "No. I can get a little wild." Brynn heated as she confessed, and she knew what the words implied. Vander seemed to sense it as well, because she blushed. And her light blue eyes drifted down to Brynn's lips and then back up again. It was an obvious look of desire. But she played it off, blinking and looking instead into the bathroom.

"Soap and towels under the sink. I'll bring your duffel and leave it by the door."

Brynn shook her head. "Wait, what?"

"Clean up here," she said, heading back down the hall. "I'm not going to let you hitchhike home. Even if I have to handcuff you to the kitchen table." She smirked and disappeared down the hall.

Brynn stared at her in disbelief. She looked back into the bathroom. Tile floor, white porcelain claw foot tub. She thought she was one of the only ones who still had one. She crossed to it and turned on the faucet. Vander's was newer, larger, nicer. It had a handheld shower head. She sat on the commode and watched the water cascade in, steam rising. Her eyes grew heavy just watching. She waited for Vander to return with her bag, but when she didn't, she turned off the water and ventured down the hallway and found her holding it, leaning against the wall, eyes closed.

"Come with me," she whispered. She took the bag and helped Vander along with her free arm. They walked back down the hall and into the largest bedroom. Brynn noted the white bed, the weathered looking blue furniture. She even liked the artwork on the wall. She sat Vander on the edge of the bed and removed her socks and flannel sleep pants. She'd bathed since she'd last seen her so her T-shirt was fresh and smelled like fabric softener. Brynn tried not to stare at her long legs or satin panties. Instead she tucked her into bed and covered her, all the while Vander mumbling things that made no sense. Brynn sat next to her and switched on the bedside lamp where a medicine bottle sat. She read the instructions, saw that it was an antibiotic, and touched Vander's cheek to wake her.

"Have you taken your antibiotic tonight?"

Vander opened heavy looking eyes. "Wha? No."

"'K. Sit up a bit." She slipped the pill in her mouth and handed her a bottle of warm water. Vander swallowed the pill and settled down into the down pillow. Gunner jumped up at the foot of the bed and settled down next to her. Brynn watched her sleep for a long moment, sighed with relief, and extinguished the light. She returned to the bathroom, stripped, and slid into the tub, groaning at the wonderful feel of the hot water. With Vander's face in her mind, she eased back and soaped herself, wishing it was Vander doing it instead of her.

Chapter Eight

K at awoke to Gunner's kisses. He was at the side of the bed, front paws resting on her pillow. His tail swept the air.

"All right, all right." She sat up, winced from her damn shoulder, and slung her legs over the bed. The medicine bottle was closed. She grabbed it, held it in her left hand, and twisted the lid with her good hand. It hurt like hell, but she got it open and popped the pill in her mouth, swallowing with tepid water. She stood and Gunner took off like a bat out of hell through her bedroom door and down the hallway.

"What's up with you, bud?" She followed him slowly, not bothering to pull on her pants. She scratched her mussed hair and turned into the living room and froze. Gunner stood at the couch, tail wagging. He barked. Brynn Williams opened her eyes and smiled, rolling over to rub Gunner's head.

"Hey, silly. It's early." She checked her watch and then noticed Kat standing there. "Oh, hi."

Kat blinked, not sure she could take in what she was seeing. Brynn was covered haphazardly with a throw blanket showing bare legs, cotton panties, and a threadbare tank top.

"Morning," Kat managed.

"I hope you don't mind my staying, but you were really exhausted and—"

"I'm glad you stayed," Kat said before she could finish. As shocked as she was to see her, it caused a mad fluttering in her chest, and she had the burning urge to smile. So much so that she couldn't help herself, and she felt it spread across her face. "I was actually going to suggest it, but I guess I sort of passed out before I got the chance."

Brynn sat up and covered her legs with the blanket. Kat saw her gaze briefly sweep up and down her half bare body, but she didn't run for cover. In fact, she liked the attention. It was rare that a beautiful woman noticed and openly admired her, especially in this town. Their eyes met, and then they both averted their gazes and seemed to struggle for words. Finally, Brynn spoke.

"How are you feeling?"

Kat glanced at her arm. "I think I'm okay. But I need to change the bandage."

Brynn studied her. "Do you need help?"

"Murph's coming by soon to do it," she said. "God knows he'll be here with bells on."

Brynn laughed. "It's nice to have someone who cares so much."

Kat cocked an eyebrow. "I never thought of it like that. I guess it is. Do you have someone like that?"

Brynn seemed surprised. "I, uh, I get by. Actually, I'm usually the one taking care of everyone else."

"I kind of figured," Kat said softly. "You are very good at it."

Brynn returned her smile. "Are you sure you don't want my services? It would save your friend a trip."

"Well, since you put it like that, how can I say no?"

Brynn shoved the blanket aside and stood. "Glad I can help." She crossed slowly to Kat, and Kat fought the urge to close her eyes and fantasize about her walking to her wearing lingerie with a look of hunger on her face.

"I'll get the stuff and meet you in the bathroom." She cleared her closing throat and looked away from her toned legs and see-through tank. The sight of her awakening nipples sent a shockwave of throbbing to her clit. She tried to force the sight from her mind, but the full package kept coming. Small, taut breasts, firm nipples, dark areolas. Smooth abdomen, long, toned legs. Pale skin, tanned in exposed areas, colliding with her thick wavy mane of auburn hair. It was enough to send her to her knees, and yet somehow she remained standing.

"You okay?" Brynn was in front of her, inches away. She reached out, touched her upper arm, and Kat felt herself inhale sharply. Embarrassed, she turned and headed for the bedroom.

"I'll meet you in the bathroom."

Kat hurried down the hallway, rethinking her decision to let Brynn help. Could she handle the close proximity? She shook it off. Of course she could. Brynn was just a nice woman offering help. She was a good person. Nothing more or less. But Kat knew it was more than that, and just because she couldn't explain it didn't mean it didn't exist. She quickly grabbed her bandaging items and hurried back down the hallway to the bathroom. Brynn was waiting inside, sitting on the edge of the tub. She'd slipped into a pair of mesh athletic shorts and pulled a worn T-shirt over her tank. The green in the shirt brought out the color in her hazel eyes, and Kat found herself inhaling again at the sight of her brushing her hair away from her brow.

"Got it," Kat said, holding up the gauze and sticky bandage. She dug under the sink, looking for where Murph had put the antibiotic ointment she was to apply. "Where the hell did he put it? You would think he would leave it with the rest of the stuff." She straightened and checked the medicine cabinet. "Got it."

She set her equipment on the counter and sat on the commode. She knew she needed to remove the sling and her shirt, and suddenly she was more than nervous. There was a tightness to the air and she sensed Brynn felt it as well.

"Tell me what to do," Brynn said softly. Her voice was low, raspy, sexy.

Kat cleared her throat. "We need to remove the sling."

Brynn moved from the tub to kneel in front of her. Kat could smell the scent of her shampoo in her hair.

"Am I hurting you?"

"Hmm?" It was becoming difficult for Kat to pay attention to words. All her other senses were on overload.

Brynn helped her out of the sling and set it aside. Then she spoke again, gently.

"Hold up your arms as best you can."

Kat did so and remembered at the last second that she wasn't wearing a bra. She'd never been ashamed of her body or shy about it before, but with Brynn she felt different. She knew if Brynn looked at her, that her own feelings of desire would be evident. Her chest was already heaving with excitement, and though she quickly covered herself with her T-shirt, she could feel her nipples tightening, yearning to be stroked.

"You okay?" Brynn asked, glancing at the T-shirt clutched to her bare chest. Brynn sounded breathless, as if she could hardly speak. "We don't have to do this."

"No, it's fine. I just—I'm just..." She rolled her eyes at herself. "I'm fine."

"I'll take your word for it," Brynn said, washing her hands thoroughly in the sink. "I understand feeling a little weird about someone you don't know very well seeing you nude." She dried her hands and turned to her and smiled. "Like when you're bathing in a creek for instance?"

Kat flushed and looked away from eyes flashing dangerously. "I'm sorry about that. I just had to make sure you were in no position to run."

"Sure." Brynn laughed and knelt in front of her again. Carefully, she pulled off the sticky bandage cover. "Was this infected?" She tugged at the gauze.

"Yes. But it should be looking better."

Brynn pulled the gauze away, her beautiful eyes focused on the wound. Kat shivered at her close proximity. She could feel her warm breath on her bare skin, and she swore she could feel a finger lightly running up her spine.

"You bled a little," she said, disposing of the used gauze. "But the wound looks okay. No pus or redness."

"Good." She would give almost anything to not have to return to the hospital. "Just wash it a little with the Dove soap and warm water. Washcloths are under the sink."

"Right."

Brynn retrieved the cloth and soap and lathered them in the sink. Then, very gently, she washed the wound. Kat winced a little but soon grew used to the sensation. She closed her eyes as Brynn finished, rinsing her with warm water and then patting her dry with a clean towel.

"Now the Polysporin," Kat said, drying her breast with the T-shirt. Brynn knelt with the tube of antibiotic ointment and a Q-tip. "Put it in the wound as best you can."

Brynn focused. "Okay."

Kat jerked a little at the contact.

"Did they remove the bullet?"

"No," she winced. "The entry was clean and the bullet was small with no spread."

"Done," Brynn said. She returned the ointment to the counter, discarded the Q-tip, and covered the wound with fresh gauze.

"Hold this here if you can," she said to Kat, taking her hand and leading her to the gauze. Kat held it, and Brynn applied the sticky bandage cover.

"All finished," she said with a smile.

"Thank you," Kat said.

Brynn eyed the T-shirt. "I take it you want to dress on your own? You're gripping that T-shirt pretty tight."

Kat realized how ridiculous she was being.

"I'm not dangerous," Brynn said with a crooked grin. "Not really."

"It's not you I'm worried about," Kat said under her breath.

Brynn cocked her head as she washed her hands again. "What?"

"Nothing." Kat slid her good arm into the T-shirt, exposing her breasts. She struggled with the bad arm. She kept her eyes on the wall and cried out when she had to raise the wounded side.

Brynn was watching her; she could feel the warmth of her gaze. And then, without a word, she stepped in front of her and helped her, talking gently to her. "There, you're as good as new." She stepped back and held out her hand.

Kat took it and stood. For a moment, they were toe-to-toe. Kat was taller, stronger. Brynn was lengthy and lean, but no doubt stronger than she looked.

"You okay?" Brynn asked again, this time a whisper.

Kat tried to look away from her penetrating gaze, but Brynn touched her hand, stopping her. Kat fought to speak, to find words and force them out, but she found instead that she was trembling and warming with both desire and the feeling of being so graciously cared for. Other than her mother, no woman had ever cared for her like this. Some had tried, but she had pushed them away. Needing help was a weakness; it showed vulnerability. But she didn't feel ashamed with Brynn. She felt...loved.

"No, I don't think I'm okay," she finally managed to say.

Brynn slid her hand completely into hers, causing Kat to shudder. "What is it? Do you hurt?"

Kat swallowed. "No."

Brynn grew closer. "Because it would kill me if you were hurting."

Kat exhaled, closed her eyes. "I can't," she said.

"Can't what?"

"Can't feel this way."

"Why?"

Kat opened her eyes.

"Because I'm a woman, or because I'm a Williams?"

Brynn reached up and held her jaw. "Tell me now, Sergeant, before I melt away in your arms right here in front of you."

Kat felt her heart jumpstart, kicking hard against her chest. She opened her mouth to speak, but Gunner barked and took off down the hall. Brynn blinked, backed away, and released her. She lowered her head as Kat walked away.

"I bet that's Murph. He didn't even give me a chance to call." Kat left Brynn behind and walked toward the living room, already hearing the locks in the front door disengaging. Gunner barked with excitement and jumped on Murph as he stepped inside. He was in full uniform so he shooed him away. Kat stood looking at him, almost pissed at him for showing up to care for her.

"Morning," he said, closing the door behind him. He held up the newspaper and tossed it on the kitchen table. "You look better and better," he said. "Did you eat? Want me to make you some eggs?"

"Murph," she said, but he didn't seem to hear.

"Margie's coming at noon to heat you up a plate and check on things. Gunner probably needs a walk. He crossed to the fridge, dug in, removing Saran Wrapped food from well-wishers to find what he wanted. He looked back at her.

"Sit down. I'll make you some livermush too. And toast. You can try Margie's mama's preserves."

"Murph," she said it louder and firmer. He stopped, frying pan in hand.

"Yeah?"

"I don't need breakfast this morning."

"No? You gotta eat, Vander. Doctor's orders, remember?"

"I'm fine and I've already had my wound cleaned too."

He set the pan down and studied her, confused. "How's that?"

"I have company," she said.

He stood in awe, trying to grasp hold of her meaning. "Company?"

"Yes. She was kind enough to clean my wound."

"Oh?" He looked shocked, disappointed. "I didn't know—I thought—"

"I know I should've called. I didn't expect you so early."

"No, it's no problem." He began returning items to the fridge. "I'm glad you have help. God knows I can't be here twenty-four seven. And Margie, with her mama and the dementia…"

"You know I appreciate you and all you do, Murph." She felt bad; he was obviously hurt.

"Yeah, I know." He closed the fridge. "She, uh, this woman, she staying with you?"

He glanced at her bare legs and large T-shirt as she ran a hand through mussed hair.

"Ye—last night—yes."

"Oh." He crossed back to the door slowly. "So no on Margie at noon?"

"Tell her thanks, but I'll be fine."

He reached for the doorknob. Gunner licked his hand and wagged his tail.

He turned. "There's no car in the drive."

Kat nodded. "I know."

He looked at her, then his face fell. "Don't tell me..." he started.

Kat held up a hand. "Murph don't."

"Brynn Williams? It's her isn't it?"

Kat started to speak, but Brynn stepped into the kitchen, surprising them both. "It's me," she said with a sad laugh. "Surprise." She forced a smile. "Don't worry. I should be going anyway."

"No," Kat said.

"I honestly didn't mean to interrupt—whatever this is," Murph said, opening the door.

"I came to get my stuff, that's all. So call off the soldiers. Vander didn't do anything wrong."

Kat looked at her. "You don't need to protect me, Brynn. It's okay."

"Brynn?" Murph said. "So you are on a first-name basis?" He shook his head. "I'll call you later, Vander." He closed the door behind him, and Kat crossed to lock it as if that would somehow erase his presence and all that had transpired.

"I'll just get my things," Brynn said. She turned and hurried after her duffel.

Kat called after her and followed. "You don't have to go."

Brynn walked toward her, duffel in hand. "I really do. I have things to straighten out at home. You need to rest, to heal. Your friends are looking out for you."

Kat wanted to stop her, to reach for her arm. She wanted to tell her to stay, that she wanted her to stay, but the words wouldn't come. Her throat was too tight with fear. Fear of rejection, fear of Murph and what he thought and what that meant. Fear that she cared what he thought.

"Brynn, you don't even have a ride."

Brynn slid into her shoes. "That won't be a problem." She held up a piece of paper. "Phone number. Ex-girlfriend."

Kat stepped back, startled. "Girlfriend?" Despite her desire and her fantasy regarding Brynn, she hadn't given serious thought to the fact that she might be gay until her words in the bathroom. Maybe it was because she wasn't known to date, too caught up in running the Williams family to care.

But here it was. She was gay and she was throwing it in her face, trying to shock her or create a reaction. And it was working.

"Yes," Brynn said. "I like women." She stuffed the paper into her pocket and headed for the door.

Kat panicked, hating the sight of her upset and leaving. "Don't."

Brynn stopped. "Why?"

"I don't want you to."

Brynn didn't turn, just stood still, facing the door. "Why?"

"Because, because…" But what could she say? She wasn't even sure her feelings were wise or safe or even rational. And Murph's reaction had told her that they might not be any of those things.

Brynn's shoulders fell. "Because you like me like I like you? I'm afraid that's not enough. I'm afraid I will never be enough. Your friend…he just pretty much said so." She laughed and looked up at the ceiling. "I'm a Williams. Lord knows that's a curse I can't do anything about. You shouldn't have to suffer because of it too." She unlocked the door and pulled it open.

"Brynn…"

"Good-bye, Vander. I would say call if you need me, but it's probably best if you didn't." She stepped out and closed the door behind her. Kat crossed to it, pulled it open, and called after her as she walked across the grass. Across the street, Murph sat in his cruiser, phone to his ear. Furious, Kat slammed the door and stormed to find her phone. She tried calling Murph, but it went straight to voice mail.

She looked out the window. Both Murph and Brynn were gone.

"Damn it." She sank into a kitchen chair, once again feeling completely helpless despite her strong will.

Gunner came to her and licked her knee. She scratched his head. "I know, Gunner. I didn't want her to go either." She stared out the window, watched a hummingbird pause to feed out of her feeder. Brynn was flying away, flying home. And her home…was just too different from hers. Unlike her own, Brynn's home would swallow her whole.

CHAPTER NINE

I suppose there's a reason as to why you're giving me a ride home?" Brynn buckled her seat belt and watched as Deputy Murphy turned down the volume to his radio, silencing the cop chatter. He accelerated and the Dodge quickened more than she expected. "You're pissed aren't you? You think she's too good for me. Well, don't worry. I won't argue with you."

They pulled onto the highway and he finally glanced over at her. "Why were you there then? Can't you just leave her alone?"

Brynn crossed her arms over her chest. "As you wish, Deputy."

He scoffed. "I'm supposed to believe that?"

She felt her face contort with anger. "Right, because Williams girls lie, right?"

He shrugged. "Your family's not exactly known for truth telling, no."

She stared him down and studied his face that looked younger than his years. But the gray coming through his closely shaved head gave him away.

"Go fuck yourself," she said. She'd had enough. She'd given in, agreed to stop seeing Vander, but it wasn't good enough. He had to add insult to injury.

He laughed. "Classy as always. Wouldn't expect anything less."

"You don't have a clue who I am. You only know my name and you're ignorant enough to think that that tells you all you need to know."

"Ignorant."

"Yes." She stared back out the window. "I don't know how Vander works with people like you."

"People like me?" He laughed again.

"You assume too much. Assume the worst in people. It's sad really. And I'm sorry you choose to live that way."

He didn't respond, and they drove in silence for a while.

"If I don't live that way, if I don't assume or expect the worst with the information I have, it can be dangerous. I could get hurt. Or worse, civilians could get hurt."

Brynn glanced at him and loosened her arms a little. He had a point, but she didn't like it. She wanted to be mad, to continue thinking he was an ignorant ass. Just another know-it-all cop. Cocky as all get-out, knew more than everyone else. She'd dealt with so many of them with the same attitude, it was difficult for her to try to see their side of things. But if she didn't, then she'd be just as ignorant as she was accusing him of being.

"I guess I can see that," she said softly.

He rubbed the back of his neck and breathed loudly. "You gotta see where I'm coming from here. You're a convicted felon. Fresh out of prison. Your sister is wanted for questioning, got a rap sheet the size of my arm, been locked up for a few months at a time. Your brother gets arrested for stealing. Both of them are into drugs. Would you want someone with all that attached to them hanging with your good friend, one you consider to be a sister?"

Brynn's eyes fell to the laptop attached to his dash. She thought long and hard. How could she defend that? She couldn't. "You're right."

"I'm not trying to be a dick here. I'm just protecting my friend. My friend who's been badly injured, my friend who might lose her partner. God, I don't know. I know how I must sound. Just—I'm sure you're nice. I mean you seem to be, but—"

"You just can't bring yourself to trust me?"

He slowed and turned on his blinker. When he spoke his voice was lower, softer. "I was hoping I didn't have to."

"Hoping I was out of the picture now."

"Are you?"

"I told her it wasn't a good idea."

His thumb jumped against the steering wheel as he rested his hand on top of it. "I think that's probably good."

"We're just too different, from different worlds."

"Right."

He drove on slowly. When he reached Williams Lane he turned and drove down the dirt road carefully. Her neighbor's dogs wandered alongside them, tails up, curious. Those neighbors that were on their front porch stared them down with unwelcome looks. Some went inside.

"You sure are popular," Brynn said. He pulled into her gravel drive and put the car in park.

"I sure am." He turned toward her. "I hope I didn't come off too badly."

"Why are you worried about it? I mean, who cares what someone like me thinks, right?" She opened her door and slung her duffel behind her shoulder. "Have a good day, Deputy," she said and shut the door.

He eased down the window and called after her. "It's for the best, Brynn. Really, it is."

She walked on, not bothering to look back. She threw back her shoulders and held her head high. She knew who she was, what was in her heart, and she wasn't going to let this guy, well-meaning or not, bring her down. She heard his tires crunch on the gravel as he backed out and turned down the lane. She crossed her overgrown lawn and climbed the steps to her porch. The familiar smell of home—cigarettes, must, and old wood—hit her before she pulled open the screen door and stepped inside. The house was sweltering.

Darkness encased her and she tossed her duffel on the couch and followed a banging noise into the kitchen. Sunlight streamed in over the sink where Billy was huddled, hitting the window air conditioner with a hammer.

Sweat glistened on his bare skin, running down into his cutoff jeans.

"Billy, what the hell are you doing?"

He jerked, caught sight of her, and blinked. "Brynn?"

He dropped the hammer in the sink and smiled, tugging at his Braves ball cap.

Brynn grinned and smacked his upper arm. "I'm back, little bro." She crossed to him and checked out the AC unit. "Aunt May just had this installed didn't she? You shouldn't be banging on it like that."

"It's not working and Bea's gone."

"Yeah, well, I'm here now."

He straightened and enveloped her in a hug. She returned it, still unable to believe how big he was. At six foot three and two thirty, Billy was built like a football player with thick shoulders and a broad back. But he'd never been interested in anything other than causing trouble. Even so, the guy had a good heart and he never intentionally hurt anyone. At least she'd instilled that in him.

"Why aren't you at work? I thought you were still helping Mr. Dudley?"

He looked down and shoved nervous hands into his pockets. "Bea said he wasn't paying me enough, so I quit." He shrugged.

"He was paying you a fair wage, Billy. I told you he would." She'd secured the job for him from inside, promised him Mr. Dudley was a good guy. Damn Bea.

"How long ago did you quit?"

Again he shrugged. "Bea said we could make more money making deliveries. But I didn't like that. The people weren't nice and they told me I might have to hurt someone if they didn't pay. They wanted me to hurt a lot of people. So I stopped doing that."

"So now you have no money?"

He shook his head.

"How long?"

"Since Bea's been gone."

Furious, Brynn crossed the room and flipped the light switches. Nothing. "Billy, the power's been cut off. That's why there's no AC. Bea hasn't paid the damn bill." She stormed into her room, so angry she could fight a room full of hornets and relish the stings. She stopped and stared. Her dressers were gone. She walked to her closet and yanked open the door. Thankfully, most of her clothes were still there. She grabbed a small flashlight, switched it on to make sure it worked, and exited. She found Billy standing in the bedroom doorway.

"Bea sold your furniture. Said we needed the money."

She rubbed her face, exasperated.

"Billy, go shower. Put on a clean shirt and shorts."

"Where we going?"

"To Nanny's tree."

"Why?"

"Just go get ready, okay?"

He walked off to shower and she went down to the dank, soil smelling basement. She again switched on the flashlight and began searching for the garden spade. She found it where she left it years ago, stuck in an old flower pot from when she'd last planted spring flowers. It was amazing how some things changed and some things didn't. As if Billy and Bea were mere ghosts sleeping and eating in the house but doing and touching little else. She turned off the flashlight and went out through the back basement door, locking it behind her. She walked across the lawn, through the big pecan trees her grandfather had planted to her great-aunt's house. She pulled open the glass weather door and knocked as she entered. Ice cold air welcomed her. May preferred it arctic cold, and Brynn always enjoyed it for the first fifteen minutes, then she always ended up hugging herself, frozen.

"May, it's Brynn!" She waited by the door taking in the smell of spice and antique furniture.

A voice came from the kitchen. "Well, I'll be, it's Brynny." Her aunt appeared and walked slowly to where she stood, arms open for an embrace. Brynn hugged her and teared up. May had always been her rock, and the thought of her getting on in years bothered her. She seemed to be shrinking, and she was feeble looking but still dressed in pressed pants and a nice blouse. Her hair was perfectly set and she still smelled the same. White Shoulders.

"How are you, young'un?"

Brynn forced a smile. "I'm okay, May. I'm okay."

May patted her abdomen. "Do they not feed you in prison?" Her crinkled eyes showed concern and she backed away offering Brynn a seat.

"Not anything you would want to eat," Brynn said, sitting on the maroon leather sofa. May sat next to her and held her hands.

"Well, are you hungry? I just made an egg salad for later. But I could make you a sandwich now."

"No, no thanks. Not right now."

May smiled and studied her closely. The woman could see things, sense things. Not a word needed to be spoken.

"What is it, child? Bea or Billy?"

Brynn sighed. "Both."

"I've been feeding Billy and he's been up here doing his wash."

"We have no power, he has no money, so that doesn't surprise me."

May patted her hand. "And Bea?"

"I have no idea. I don't know where she is. Apparently, she got Billy into delivering drugs. So he quit his job. His good job. Now he's got nothing, and he's been living that way since Bea came to get me."

"I don't know what all's been going on. I've been telling you as much as I can. You know Bea doesn't come up here since I stopped giving her money. And Billy, he comes, but he won't tell me things."

"I know." Brynn closed her eyes. "I appreciate what you do. We'd be lost without you."

May watched her. "What else, honey. A policeman? I saw one bring you in. Got all the phones a ringing around here."

Brynn pressed her lips together. "That, Aunt May, is a story for another day. Right now, I need to borrow your Lincoln to go get some money and pay some bills, get some food."

"Of course." She smiled. "You know where the keys are. Are you sure you won't have a sandwich?"

Brynn kissed her cheek. "Later, I promise. Billy and I will come eat with you."

Brynn crossed to the kitchen to retrieve the keys. When she returned, she hugged May again and exited to her front porch. The mosquitoes were already out, floating around the lawn ornaments, seeking, searching, like little sharks. She smacked her legs as she opened the old Lincoln's large door, tossed in the spade, and slid inside to start the engine. She backed out and drove to her house where she honked for Billy. He came out and jogged to the car, tugging on his ball cap. When he climbed in she could smell the Irish Spring on him.

"You going to tell me why we're going to Nanny's tree?"

She put the car in gear and drove up Williams Lane. "To get some money."

"There's money at Nanny's tree?"

"There is."

He sat back and didn't ask any more questions, and she didn't offer any more information. The money had been her well-kept secret and she'd promised to never tell anyone about it and to only use it in emergencies. Her Nanny had left it to her when she'd died, and Brynn had been smart enough to bury it out where her grandmother had grown up. Far away from Bea.

When she pulled into the old Holland homestead, she crept down the dirt road, hoping those who now lived on the property wouldn't give them any trouble. Their mobile homes were off in the distance, so she hoped to be in and out. Billy stirred, having fallen asleep on the ride over.

"We here?" He rubbed his eyes.

"Mm hm." Brynn grabbed the garden spade and climbed from the car. Billy did the same. The tree in front of them was a large willow. Her grandmother had always claimed it's where she would run to when she needed time to think. As a child, she'd buried things there. Trinkets, toys, anything she wanted to hide from her siblings. So it had only been natural for Brynn to think of the tree when she needed to hide the money.

Tears burned her eyes as Brynn located the spot and sank to her knees. She reached up to trace her grandmother's initials in the bark. Then, as Billy sank down next to her, she dug. The earth was soft, the dirt red. She dug until she hit tin and stopped. With Billy's help they scooped the dirt away and exposed the old tin lunchbox. Brynn laughed.

"Remember this?" She lifted the Smurfs lunchbox and brushed it off.

Billy nodded. "That was Emily's wasn't it?"

"Sure was." Emily, their older cousin, had always given them her hand-me-downs. Including the lunchbox.

Brynn set the box on the ground and unlatched the rusted locks. She popped the lid and sighed with relief.

"Thank God." She looked to the sky. "Thank you."

"How much is that?" Billy asked, sweat trickling down his temples.

"Never you mind," she said. "Enough. And that's all that matters."

They stood and hurried back to the car. Brynn kept the box in her lap and drove back down the road. Quickly, she pulled back on the main road and sped toward town. Billy made waves with his arm out the window, playing with the hot air. She watched him and wiped away a tear. He was so naïve, so sweet. He'd tested low in school and she'd had to put him on a different bus every morning so he could go to the school that better met his needs. She'd worried about him constantly for as long as she could remember while Bea had taken him under her wing and used him to carry out things she didn't want to do herself. It infuriated Brynn, but Billy couldn't see it and he loved Bea so much.

"I'm going to call tonight and get your job back, okay?"

Billy smiled. "Okay."

"Billy?"

He looked at her. "Yeah?"

"You still doing drugs?"

His eyes fell and he looked regretful, like he felt ashamed about her asking. "No. Not in a long time. I don't like how I feel when I can't get them."

She nodded. "Good. Now you know what I mean when I say they aren't good."

"Yeah. But Bea does. Her and Robbie, they do a lot of bad things. You would be mad. And I don't want you mad at me."

She reached over and patted his leg. "I'm not mad at you, Billy. I just worry. I just wish you would listen to me rather than Bea."

He looked back out the window. "I think I should too. I think you love me more."

Brynn blinked at him. Maybe he understood more than she thought.

"Where's your mountain bike?" He always got around town on his bike. He loved the freedom it gave him.

"Bea sold it."

Brynn clenched her jaw. "Okay." She tried to sound lighthearted. "We'll get you another one."

"Really?" He lifted his ball cap and scratched his hairline.

"Sure. You gotta get around, right? And we'll get you a good lock and you can lock it up at home too where Bea and her friends can't get it."

He smiled, pulled down his ball cap, and once again made waves in the air with his arm. Brynn drove on thinking about Bea. She wondered where she was and where she'd left the car. If she was smart she would cross the state line and hide out somewhere far away. But Bea didn't like leaving home and rarely ventured from the county. Big cities overwhelmed her. She liked rural areas and old farmhouses on acres of land. She'd once said she'd never leave Williams Lane. Brynn hoped she was okay, but more than anything, she hoped she'd turn herself in for her own sake. Her current situation was dangerous, and Brynn didn't want her getting hurt or causing anyone else to get hurt.

She breathed deeply as she thought about Vander's partner and what Deputy Murphy had said. Deputy Damien might not survive. Brynn cringed as a wave of guilt overcame her. Why didn't she check his pulse? Why didn't she make sure he was dead?

Maybe he would've had a better chance if she'd dragged him to the car too. But he'd looked dead, bullet wound to the head. She wrung her hands along the steering wheel. She felt responsible, and she hated thinking about how badly his loss would hurt Vander.

She swallowed around a tightening throat as she entered town and slowed to pull into the power company to pay the bill. She wished there was something she could do. She had to make it right or the guilt would eat her alive. She just wasn't sure what she could do.

Billy climbed out of the car with her.

"I have a lot to do the next week or so," she said to Billy. "But we will definitely get you a new bike, okay?"

He nodded and they opened the door to clean up yet another one of Bea's messes. Was this how the rest of her life was going to play out?

CHAPTER TEN

K at walked into the hospital, clenching her fist in nervousness. It felt like the hundredth time she'd come to see Damien, but it didn't seem to matter when it came to her nerves. The first time she'd had to insist on coming, insisting Margie drive her. When she'd entered Damien's room she'd gasped and backed up, completely unprepared for what she'd seen. His wife, Genie, had come to her, grabbed her hand, and led her to a chair. Damien was lifeless, machine pushing in breath after breath, hissing. His head was shaven, wrapped partially in a bandage. His chest rose and fell with the hissing.

"No one told me," Kat had said. "Oh God, no one told me."

She'd lit into her captain and Murph both that evening when she'd gotten home. Why hadn't they told her how serious he was? She'd been asking and asking about him, but they had only told her he was still healing. They'd said that they were trying to protect her, to allow her to heal a little first. While she understood their intent, she didn't agree with it. What if Damien had died? She wouldn't have had the chance to tell him good-bye.

Damien had been her close friend for ten years. They'd been fast friends since the first day they'd met in the gym, both of them grunting louder than the others as they pushed themselves beyond limits. Their fellow officers laughed and gave them a hard time. Kat had looked at Damien and shrugged.

"Jealousy's a disease," she'd said to the others. "Get well soon, fellas." She then high-fived Damien as he laughed and introduced himself.

They'd been nearly inseparable ever since, and when Damien had been assigned to work with her, a bond had formed. One of mutual respect and caring and something that went deeper. She watched his back, made sure he made it home to his wife and kids. She'd been there for his wedding, the birth of his kids. She'd rescued a dog and given it to his kids for Christmas, much to his dismay, which had only made her and Genie laugh. She loved him. He was blood. Family. And no one was allowed to fuck with that.

She pushed the button for the elevator and rotated her shoulder, finally free of the sling. She'd already started a little physical therapy, which she hated. But she did it anyway, pushing through the frustration, the setbacks, her need for perfection. She had always excelled, and it wasn't easy to see her body so weak and unable to function properly. Damien would give her such shit if he could see her lose her temper at therapy. The thought made her laugh and then tear up. He would have to wake up first.

The elevator door opened and she stepped in. A woman with balloons and flowers entered, taking up most of the space. Kat had done the same on the first visit, but today she brought him his favorite—banana pudding. Even if he wasn't awake, she believed he could hear her, and she was damn sure gonna let him know that she and Genie were enjoying it without him. If that didn't get to him and make him wake up, nothing would.

She politely pushed past the balloons and stepped out at her floor. She walked quickly with her typical long strides. The closer she came to his room, the more nervous she grew. Sweat formed at her hairline and dripped down the back of her neck. Seeing him hooked up to all those machines scared the shit out of her. He looked so pale, thin. Gaunt. It was like watching helplessly as your dear brother slipped away, tethered to life by cords hooked to machines. She prayed he'd hang on, hang on tight to those tethers.

She came to his room, gave a few nurses at their circular counter a wave, and pushed open the cracked door to enter. But she heard a voice, a familiar voice, and she halted to listen. Her heart pounded as she heard Brynn Williams speak to Genie.

"I'm just so sorry. I should've done more. Should've thought to do more. He just looked so bad and he didn't move...I'm just so sorry. It's my fault he's so bad off. I could've got him help a lot sooner." She grew quiet and then Kat could hear her stifle back sobs.

Genie spoke, and Kat could see her cross the room to where Brynn must be standing. Kat pushed the door open a little farther and saw them embrace. She took in a quick breath, the sight moving her deep inside.

"Don't you burden yourself with this," Genie said through tears. "You did the best you could. Lord knows what you went through just helping the way you did. Honestly, after I saw the dash cam footage, I can't believe Kat or Brian are alive at all."

"I could've done more," Brynn said. Kat saw them pull apart, and Genie brushed Brynn's hair from her face.

"He's alive. He's alive because of you." She smiled softly. "Thank you for that."

Brynn wiped her eyes, then dug in her jeans pocket. She pulled out a folded stack of money and tried to press it to Genie's palm. "This is all I can do," she said. "God knows if I could wake him up, I would. But I can't."

"Brynn, please, no. I can't take this."

"Please do. I know you have children, a home to care for. This will help a little."

Genie held her forearms. "Trust me, we are well cared for. We are loved. Damien…he means so much to a lot of people."

Brynn eventually nodded and shoved the bills back into her pocket. "If you ever need anything, you'll call me?"

"I will," Genie said. "But please don't be a stranger. Stay awhile. Visit often. He can hear us. I believe that with everything I am."

Brynn and Genie crossed to Damien. Brynn took his hand and sat. Genie stood, hand on her shoulder. Brynn massaged his hand and Kat heated, knowing she should look away, but she couldn't. She couldn't tear her eyes away from the tender moment.

Just then she felt a hand touch her shoulder from behind. "Excuse me," a nurse said pushing a machine. "I need to check on him."

Kat moved aside, exposing her presence. Genie smiled.

"Kat, you're back so soon." She greeted the nurse with a pat to her arm and left Brynn sitting with Damien. Genie enveloped her in a warm hug. "It's good to see you." Her eyes were red rimmed and puffy, her face pale and hollow. She'd done a lot of crying and praying, and it was beginning to show.

"I can't seem to stay away," Kat said, trying to sound casual. "He's never going to get rid of me you know."

Genie laughed. "I'm sure he's aware of that."

"He better be," Kat said, stepping farther in the room. She handed over the container of pudding. "Banana," she said. "His favorite."

"Oh my Lord, you didn't. Babe, you hear that? Banana pudding." She placed it on a bed table and offered Kat a seat. "Kat, do you know…of course you do," Genie said, catching herself.

Kat met Brynn's gaze. She could feel her heartbeat in her ears. It had been almost two weeks since she'd seen her, and she looked as beautiful as ever, in loose jeans and a white polo style shirt. Her thick hair hung below her shoulders and reflected waves of auburn in the sunlight coming in through the blinds. She offered a smile, but it fell quickly. She gently released Damien's hand and stood.

"I should go."

Genie glanced at Kat in surprise. "You don't have to you know. You're welcome here."

"I know, I just have errands, and my brother…"

"No, don't go," Kat said softly. But Brynn wouldn't look at her and she was smiling, but Kat could tell it was for Genie only.

"I'm afraid I have to go." She and Genie squeezed hands. "Thanks for letting me visit and for…accepting me, you know, with my history, and—"

"What you did shows who you are," Genie said. "That's all that matters to me."

Brynn nodded and gave a half smile. "I wish it were that way with most." There was a pause, a heavy silence. "I'll keep praying for you all," Brynn said. She left Genie and glanced up at Kat as she walked by. "Shoulder feeling better?"

Kat watched her and she wanted to speak, but she wasn't going to stop to listen. "Yes," Kat said as Brynn walked out the door. Without a second's hesitation, Kat went after her. This was the second time she'd seen her leave, and it tore at her just as it had the first time. And for the second time, she felt powerless in stopping her.

"Brynn, wait." Kat jogged to her, catching her before she reached the elevator. The movement hurt her injury, but she winced it away.

Brynn stopped and turned. She looked shell-shocked and anxious. Like a rabbit frozen in the gaze of an approaching predator. She didn't speak, just glanced at her a few times but ended up averting her gaze.

"Thanks," Kat said, standing next to her. "For stopping."

"How can I help you, Sergeant?" She crossed her arms over her chest, and Kat knew she was protecting herself. She was obviously still hurt about their last encounter when she'd decided they shouldn't see each other. It had hurt Kat, but she'd respected her wishes, not wanting to cause her any pain or do anything she didn't want.

"Why won't you look at me?"

Brynn did and the gaze nearly floored her it was so cold.

"Are you upset with me? Have I done something, said something?"

Brynn bit on her lower lip. "No."

"Okay…then please tell me what it is."

Brynn shook her head. "It's nothing. I just shouldn't be here. This is your family, friends. Not mine. I just feel responsible and I feel so bad about him, and—" She started to cry. She turned and covered her mouth. Her shoulders shook. But just as quickly, she straightened and took a deep breath. Kat touched her shoulder which made her jerk with surprise.

"You are not responsible," Kat said. She lifted her hand. "I am."

Brynn turned and faced her with watery eyes. "You?"

Kat felt her own tears come. She had to clear her throat to talk. "I, uh, I have these dreams about it, you know? And I see him there and he can't take cover because of his seat belt. He tried to get it off, but they fired at him first, then me. I tried, I tried so hard to get him down. But I didn't. I failed him. I failed his family and friends." Kat turned, not wanting to cry in front of her. She rarely cried, rarely caved, and she was upset at herself for doing so in public. She had to be strong, for Genie, for Damien, for everyone. If she lost it she feared they'd all lose hope, or worse, baby her more and keep things from her. As if she were too weak to handle things because she was female. She'd always resented it and so she'd steeled herself to face anything without emotion. It was one of the reasons why she was so good at her job. Now here she was losing it in the hospital in front of the first woman she'd been drawn to in a long while.

"Are you okay?" Brynn asked.

Kat wiped her cheeks and turned to put on a smile. "Yes, I'm fine."

"It's not your fault either," Brynn said softly. She was looking at her with such concern, almost as if she wanted to touch her. She even lifted her hand, but then dropped it along with her gaze. "You shouldn't blame yourself." The soft look was gone, vanished just as quickly as it had come.

"Yeah, well, easier said than done." They stood in silence for a moment. Kat wanted to ask her to go for coffee after her visit with Damien to get both their minds on happier things, or to dinner later that evening where they could have a beer and relax. But it was obvious Brynn wanted nothing to do with her. And as emotional as Kat was already feeling, she didn't want to risk being rejected on top of it.

"I need to get going," Brynn said. She walked to the elevators with Kat right on her heels.

"Damn it, will you just wait?" Kat felt lost, helpless. "Why are you being so cold with me?"

Brynn laughed. "As if you don't know."

Kat blinked. "Know what?"

Brynn shook her head and pressed the down button. "Nothing."

"Brynn, please."

"Why do you care? I mean why care what I'm thinking or feeling?"

Kat fought for words. "Because I care."

"You care?" Brynn looked at her in disbelief.

"Yes."

"I see. You care, but from a safe distance, right? Safer that way?" She nodded. "You're right, it is safer. After all, I'm contagious. And the bacteria of trouble that follows me around might somehow rub off on you."

"What?" Kat studied her, trying to follow her meaning.

A ding sounded and the elevator opened. After a couple of people in scrubs exited, Brynn stepped in. "There's someone down the hall who needs your caring. Go to him and don't worry about me."

The door slowly closed, and Kat was left at a loss. She had no idea what had just transpired. It was as if Kat had said something to her about her family or her status. But Kat had said nothing, only followed her wishes.

Shouting came from down the hall, and nurses scrambled, two running into Damien's room. Genie stepped out of the door and called to her.

"Kat, he's waking up!"

Kat took off down the hall, Brynn Williams still tucked in her mind.

Chapter Eleven

B rynn hurried around the house, carrying the ironing board, wearing her good jeans and a black lace bra. She entered her room and set up the ironing board and placed the already steaming iron on the end. Her wet hair was wound up in a towel, and music blared from an old handheld radio she'd found in the basement. Thankfully, she had music and her favorite shirt was still in the back of her closet. It was a lavender button-up, and everyone loved how it looked against her hair.

She ironed the shirt and wiped the sweat from her brow. She left the board to stand in front of the box fan. The AC was working, but they really needed two units to cool the entire house. But that was a problem for another day. Tonight was hers. She was in bad need of a break, and she'd decided she was going out, come hell or high water. She had called Holly after her visit to the hospital and they'd decided to drive to Charlottetown and hit a bar. Holly was still upset about her missing car, but she knew it wasn't Brynn's fault. She'd actually been excited in hearing from her, and she'd been more than willing to go to the city for the night. Brynn knew she was probably hoping for more than a drink and a dance, but Brynn didn't care. She wasn't going to worry about it. The woman she wanted she couldn't have, and there was no sense in crying over it. It was just the way things were. A cop and a Williams just didn't go together. Everyone seemed to believe that but her. Even her own family and neighbors had commented on the cop who had dropped her off. They didn't want them around, and Brynn had to assure them it wasn't going to be a regular thing.

She plugged in her hair dryer and stood in front of her floor-length mirror to do her hair. She decided to wear it down and, pleased with how it looked, she started in on her makeup. She didn't wear a lot. Just enough to accent her eyes and accentuate her lips. She was blessed with a good complexion and didn't need much foundation either. When she finished, she sprayed on a unisex cologne, and slipped into her shirt, leaving it unbuttoned low enough to see winks of her bra. Then she stepped into her leather ankle boots and laced them up. She switched off her radio, turned off the iron and light, and breezed by Billy in the living room on the way out.

"I'll be back tomorrow," she said, having already discussed her night out with him.

"Okay." He waved at her, never taking his eyes off the television. "Have fun."

"I will!" She was determined to, and she smiled as she pushed out the screen door and hurried down the steps to Holly who sat waiting in her old Nova.

"Come on, girl, let's get outta here!" She revved the engine and laughed as Brynn climbed in. "Mm, you smell yummy." She leaned over to kiss her, and Brynn pushed her away, causing more laughter. "Aw, come on, a kiss for the ride?" She backed up and drove up the dirt road.

"We'll see," Brynn said, buckling her lap belt. She smiled at Holly. "You look nice."

"Why, thank you." She smoothed down her black v-neck tee. Her blond hair was pulled back in a tight pony-tail. Her jeans were faded blue, almost white and skinny fit. She gave her a wink. "You look hot. I always liked that shirt."

"Thanks. It's about the only nice thing I've got left."

"Well, girl, you sure can wear it. And hopefully not for long."

Brynn laughed. "From your lips to God's ears." She needed to get a little wild, have crazy passionate sex with a like-minded woman. She could already imagine the release, over and over again.

She settled back and closed her eyes as Holly pulled on the highway. The car was loud and she could smell the gasoline. She loved it and ran her hands over the black vinyl seats. Holly had had the car since high school, and they'd made out more than once in the backseat.

"Thinking about old times?" Holly asked.

"Mm."

Holly looked in the rearview mirror and changed lanes. "Why didn't we ever get serious? We get along so well, and the sex, it wasn't half bad."

"We deserve better than half bad."

Holly looked over at her. "I just worry I'm never gonna find anyone."

"No one is better than someone who's wrong. We've both learned that lesson."

"Don't you ever wonder if you'll find the one?"

Brynn stared out the window into the twilight. "I think I already did."

"What? Who?"

Brynn shook her head. "No one you know."

"So why aren't you with her? She in prison?"

Brynn laughed. "No. She...she's a cop."

Brynn watched as Holly's jaw dropped. "Say what? No way. Not Brynn Williams. Jesus, ya'll all hate the police. And after you went down for Bea, I thought you'd hate the whole lot of them."

"I've never really had anything against the police," Brynn said. "I got upset when they came around because they were usually bringing me a stoned Bea or a shoplifting Billy. I was never pissed at the cops."

"Have you told anyone else? Because they're gonna shit."

Brynn looked down at her hands in defeat. She suddenly felt hollow inside, and the thought of having fun began to dissipate. "Her friend sort of let me know he didn't approve either."

"You're kidding."

"No. And it's for the best really. At least I think it is. That's what everyone says anyway."

"What do you say?"

"I say…I wish I lived a different life in a different world where my name and family didn't matter. Where I didn't have to worry about my name and my family. Where I could be free. Free to fly. Fly to her and be with her." She closed her eyes again and let the warmth of that thought overcome her. "I just want to fly, fly far away."

❖

Blush was crowded. Brynn awoke to a honking horn and a cussing Holly.

"That's my space!"

Brynn straightened and tried to check herself in the rear-view mirror as Holly swung into the one and only parking spot left. "I slept the whole way?" She didn't remember falling asleep, and she felt kind of bad about it. Holly had to drive the forty-five minutes in silence since the Nova no longer had a functioning radio.

"Just about," she said, nudging Brynn over for her own once-over in the mirror.

Brynn climbed from the car and stretched. Night had completely fallen and yet it was still muggy as hell. Cars huddled in lines, and behind the lot, lightning bugs hung in the air. Brynn looked up for the clouds. She smelled rain.

"It's gonna pour isn't it?"

"This late?" Holly waved her off. "I wouldn't say pour."

"I bet it does," Brynn said, seeing no stars. Holly was right. In the summer, storms usually came in the afternoon. But she had a feeling about this one. It was definitely brewing, having built up for so long, biding its time. It was damn near ready to burst.

"I bet it doesn't." Holly walked by her side as they headed for the door. "I'll bet you a fine cigar it doesn't."

Brynn shook her hand. "You're on."

The live music could be heard before they hit the door. Blush shown in red neon over the door of the old brick building. Years ago it had been a warehouse, then a sports bar, and now...the gays had taken control. Brynn smiled as they walked in, loving the music, the space, the low light. She held on to Holly's back as they headed for the bar. The inside was plush with deep purples and reds. Tables circled the large dance floor and lounges were toward the back. Black-and-white photos hung on the wall, the owner an avid photographer. She sometimes walked the floor, asking people to come sit for her. She had a good eye for models. Brynn loved looking at the photos of the beautiful models with angled jaws, high cheekbones, and wicked eyes. One of the photos, one of a blonde with slicked back hair, actually looked a lot like Kat Vander. She pointed to it and started to say something, but Holly pointed toward the stage where a small indie band from the area was playing. Brynn had heard them before. Their lyrics were dark, brooding, vampire-ish. Four women singing about sucking on another woman's skin, yep, that did it for her. And she guessed it did it for the others as well since they were back performing.

She bounced next to Holly and placed her elbows on the bar. "What should we have?" she asked her.

Holly was bobbing her head, grinning. She grabbed her head and yelled in her ear. "Tequila!"

"No kidding?"

Holly jumped up and down. "Yes, let's do it."

Brynn ordered, shook off the Cuervo, and pointed to the Patron. They took their two shots each, found the salt and waited for the limes. They did the first two shots back-to-back and danced. Brynn signaled for another. Her face started to warm as they did the third one.

"I can't even taste it," Holly said.

Brynn paid and led her to the dance floor. They searched the crowd, like sharks waiting for the scent of blood. There were many attractive women, but Brynn found that she really didn't want to dance with any of them. Instead, she took Holly's hand and led her out under the lights. Her buzz was coming full on and she felt so good, so light, so warm. She moved into her and they throbbed with the others, in sync with the lights. Holly kept throwing her arms up in the air and yelling. Brynn laughed and did it with her a few times. They danced to song after song, and soon the lights dimmed even more and the strobes slowed as the lead singer cuffed the mic and belted out lyrics with low, deep music.

"How about that kiss now?" Holly asked.

Brynn leaned into her. "What?"

"That kiss you owe me." She laughed, and before Brynn could stop her, she had pulled her in and planted her mouth on hers, seeking with her tongue. For a split second Brynn fell into it, having not had any human contact in four years. But Holly was going too far, grabbing her ass and holding her fast while she tried to swallow her whole.

Brynn finally managed to pull away. She started to yell at her, but she saw a face behind her. It was spotlighted in blue, light, slicked back hair, angled jaw, high cheekbones. Brynn inhaled sharply as her heart flooded with hot blood. Kat Vander was standing there, skin ashen, hard look on her face. Holly caught Brynn's stare and turned. Vander eyed her, then looked back to Brynn.

The singer crooned out dark words. Words that penetrated, piercing Brynn's heart, making her bleed.

Your clit, sharp and dangerous,
Slices into my mouth,
Making me bleed
Hot blood. I drink
With your hot come
And I swallow, and
Swallow, and
Fucking fly, touch the ceiling
With you, as you come
As I feed...

The crowd was silent, hanging on every word. Someone whistled and Vander seemed to awaken to her reality. She turned and hurried toward the lounges where there was an exit.

"I have to go," Brynn said. "Don't wait for me."

She left Holly with questions and ran after Vander, winding through the crowd. She grabbed her good arm and pulled her to the wall in the darkness.

"Don't," Vander said, turning to glare at her. "Just don't."

Brynn could barely make out the angles of her goddess like face in the dim light. But she was able to see the hurt. The pain. She couldn't bear it, not on her and not in herself.

Not anymore. She shoved her against the wall, harder, tighter.

"I have to," she said. She could feel Vander's heartbeat beneath her palm. It was racing, competing with her own.

The lyrics finally ended and the crowd roared. Brynn pressed closer.

"What do you want?" Vander asked, voice high with emotion. "Just tell me what you want, Brynn Williams."

Brynn leaned close to her ear and said what she'd wanted to say for so long. "To make you come."

Brynn felt her shiver, felt the moist sweat of her skin against her cheek. And then, as quick as lightning, Vander latched onto her, tugged her in close. She kissed her neck, sucked, licked. Brynn groaned, her own skin dimpling from the sensation of a hot mouth. She fell into her, grinding herself against her strong thigh. They were heated, panting, out of control. Words were spoken, rasped, ragged.

"My God, you taste good," Vander said, nibbling her ear. "I could eat you alive."

Brynn laughed and then her breath caught. It felt so good, her words, her want, just for Brynn. Vander was alive and craving, Brynn her meal. She never could've imagined this kind of unabashed hunger from her. It nearly overtook her, nearly made her come in her jeans. The mere thought made her pulse against her, and she found that she was unable to control the urgent kick in her hips.

"Ride me," Vander said, sending another bolt of desire down her spine. Vander cupped her ass, pulled her tighter, helping her thrust against her.

Hurriedly, wanting her to feel the same, Brynn lowered her hand and pressed into Vander's crotch, causing her to cry out softly. She was moist, swollen, and she threw her head back against the wall.

She was caught up and they were stuck together like wild beings tearing at one another. The thought must've reached her because she began to worry.

"Shit—someone's gonna see us," Vander said, her voice trembling. Still, they did not stop.

"It's dark," Brynn said. She went in and bit her neck, causing her to jerk and groan. "But we can stop if you want." She pressed her harder, gliding her fingers up and down.

Vander whispered. "Ah, fuck no, don't stop."

"Then come in my hand," Brynn said, breathless. "Come right here, right now. Come with me."

Vander made a deep noise of pleasure as their mouths met for the first time. Brynn moaned at the feel of her soft, full lips, pressing, framing her own. They teased, not fully committing, pressing, breathing, pulling back. Brynn closed her eyes, feeling her breath, and then the wet tease of her tongue. Brynn teased back, and soon, with wild abandon, they fell into a beautiful, hot rhythm, kissing completely, fully, devouring. Brynn gripped Vander's neck never wanting to let go. But the mounting pressure on her engorged clit caused her to tear away and throw back her head as her cunt came alive and pulsed, demanding to be released. They moved, harder, faster, and Brynn knotted her hand in her hair, looked into her eyes. Vander nearly lifted her off the ground with one arm.

Brynn could feel the harnessed power of her body, and she knew as wild as this was, she was holding back.

"Tell me you'll take me somewhere and have your way with me."

Vander breathed rapidly and touched her lips with her mouth. She spoke. "You read my mind."

"Good," Brynn breathed, "because I'm going to come." She bit the edge of her jaw, moaned, and came. Vander followed, burying her head in her neck, calling out into her flesh. They rocked and fucked and came in a series of shivers and death grips, in the darkness, where cries and sighs get absorbed by the black and loud, like creatures of the night. They clung to one another, moving together, grunting softly, until Brynn was nearly too weak to stand. She collapsed and Vander held to her, breathing hard. Brynn felt her heart catapult upon itself in her chest as she rested against her.

"Brynn," Vander finally said, cupping the back of her head.

Brynn could hardly move. Barely speak. "Sergeant."

"I have to get you alone before I get us arrested."

"Can't move." Brynn clung to her loosely, hypnotized by her heartbeat.

"Come on." Vander wrapped an arm around her waist and led them through the side door. They moved slowly, freshly fucked, bodies spent, in a daze. Rain pelted their scalp and skin. Brynn laughed, so relaxed, feeling so good. She looked up at the sky, at the beautiful maze of falling rain. The storm, like her, had finally burst and let it all out.

CHAPTER TWELVE

Kat watched Brynn laugh up into the rain. Her skin glistened, slick and beautiful in the glow of the streetlight. Kat grew breathless once again, her insides ready to burst and fill her with yearning, desire, hunger, needs she desperately wanted to feed.

She tugged her closer and led them to her car. She opened the passenger door and Brynn caught her with an arm around the neck. She kissed her, and Kat fell into the feel of the cold rain layered against Brynn's hot skin. They melded together, and Kat pushed into her with her tongue, once, twice, three times. She groaned as her clit began to demand more and she forced herself away, too excited to continue.

"Let's go," she said, touching Brynn's face. She could see the streetlight reflected in her gaze. The light was sparking, striking to life, breathing with desire. Kat could've stared into it for hours.

Brynn grinned and Kat wanted to kiss her, but instead she rounded the car and climbed in to start the engine. Brynn glanced over at her as they fled the parking lot. "Where are you taking me, Sergeant Vander?" She reached over and toyed with the back of her neck. It caused shivers to run right through her. Brynn still had the grin, and if Kat could bottle that look, that image of her seducing her from the passenger seat of her car, she'd die a happy woman.

"To a hotel." It took all she had to refocus on the road. She wiped rain from her face and stared through the windshield wipers. Brynn continued to tease the back of her neck with nimble fingers. "I, uh, reserved one for tonight."

"Thought you'd get lucky did you?"

Kat laughed. "I'd hoped, didn't you?"

"I did. But I never could've imagined this."

Kat gave her a glance. "I'd imagined it plenty. I just never thought it would happen."

Brynn looked away and her fingers stopped their teasing. Kat worried for a split second that something was wrong, but just as quickly, Brynn reassured her.

"You imagined it?" Her fingers moved to her jaw where they traced lightly.

Kat swallowed hard. "Oh yeah."

"Was I wearing black lace?" She retracted her hand. "Like this?"

Kat looked over and saw her unbutton her lavender shirt and run her fingers along the edges of a see-through black lace bra.

Kat breathed deeply. "No, but you will from now on." She gripped the steering wheel and inwardly swore at the red light. The hotel seemed to be a million miles away.

Brynn laughed. "You really think about me like this?"

Kat heated. "Yes."

"I do too," Brynn said softly. "For a while now." She reached over, took Kat's hand, kissed it, lightly breathed upon her palm, and then snuck out her tongue to run along her inner wrist.

"Brynn, you better stop. We won't make it."

"Drive faster."

"Christ, I am."

"Faster." Brynn took her finger in her mouth and sucked.

Kat sped up and fought closing her eyes in sheer pleasure. Her toes curled in her shoes, and she clenched her legs together as her clit awoke once again. Up ahead, the hotel came into view and the tires squealed as she slammed on the brakes and took the turn-in too fast. But she didn't care and Brynn only laughed. She pulled her hand away, parked, and killed the engine.

They sat in silence. Kat fought for breath. "That was evil," she said.

"I told you I could be a little wild sometimes."

Kat smiled. "I can believe it."

Brynn buttoned up her shirt. "You gonna take me inside, Sergeant?"

Kat studied her slender fingers working the buttons. Studied the slick wet skin of her neck and face. Honed in on her dark lips and electrifying eyes. Her cheeks were tainted red atop her high cheekbones. A raindrop fell from a strand of hair onto her face, and she brushed it aside in a move that left Kat breathless.

"I am," Kat finally said. She threw open her door and met Brynn at the back of the car. She took her hand and hustled them inside. They jogged to the elevator, soaking wet, ignoring the glances from curious onlookers.

Brynn leaned in and whispered in her ear. "Ever fuck in an elevator?"

Kat squeezed her hand. "No. Have you?"

"No."

"They have cameras in them now."

"Really?" Brynn seemed intrigued.

Kat smiled. "You're really bad, aren't you?"

"You're bringing out a whole new, more dangerous side to me."

"I'm not sure if that's good or bad."

The doors slid open and they stepped inside. Brynn lowered her voice as Kat pressed the number for their floor. "It's very good for you. If you're into it."

"I can't imagine you doing anything in the bedroom that I'm not into."

"Sergeant, you continue to surprise me."

"Do I?"

"Yes."

They grew closer, breathed into one another as they came dangerously close to a kiss.

The elevator stopped and the doors opened. Kat tugged on her and led them to her room. She slid in the card key and opened the door. Brynn held her eyes as she entered, already unbuttoning her shirt once again. Kat closed and locked the door and approached her, stopping at the foot of the bed. The room was quiet, white duvet-covered bed, patterned sofa and chairs near the door to the patio. A vase of fresh flowers sat on the coffee table.

"Don't you want to get out of those wet clothes?" Brynn asked in a husky voice, stopping to inhale the flowers. She chose a daisy and crossed to Kat. She stroked her bare chest with the flower, down to her navel where her shirt remained buttoned.

"I don't want to miss a moment of watching you."

Brynn grinned, stepped up, and pressed her onto the bed. Kat sat, Brynn between her legs. Brynn stroked her face with the flower, her jaw, her neck.

"I'm going to put my mouth everywhere this flower touches." The flower continued downward, across her navel to her jeans. Brynn paused and looked at her. "Do you want me to go lower?"

Kat swallowed as she watched the flower move up and down her fly. With every stroke, a gush of arousal warmed her panties. She began to rock her hips despite being unable to feel the delicate touch of the flower. "Yes," she breathed.

"Oh yes, you want my mouth here, don't you?" She moved the flower lower, twisted the stem so the flower flattened and engrossed her crotch in playful circles. "You want my mouth all over you down here, don't you?"

Kat grabbed her wrist. "Yes." Her head was spinning, and she was so used to being in control she wasn't sure what was happening. She held her wrist, needing to stop, to gain her bearings. She needed to throw Brynn on the bed and have her way with her, but she couldn't move, didn't want to move. Brynn was playing her, teasing her, like a marionette does a puppet, and Kat was so wet she was sure she had saturated the duvet.

Brynn pushed on her shoulder, encouraging her to lean back on her elbows. "You don't know what to say do you? You're so used to being the top." She laughed. "But you can't seem to fight me can you?"

Kat could feel her own pulse beat in her neck, in her ears. "No."

"When you thought of me, you thought of taking me, didn't you?"

Kat nodded.

"You had no idea that it would be me, shoving you up against the wall and pushing you back on the bed, did you?"

"No."

"I surprised you," Brynn said, twirling the flower across her lips, tongue sneaking out to taste one petal after another.

"Yes."

She stared into Kat and tossed the flower aside. She leaned forward and whispered while straddling Kat's leg. "I'm going to give you so much more than your fantasies, Sergeant."

She straightened and stripped out of her shirt slowly, showing her lean, lithe body in the black lace bra.

"My God," Kat said, unable to tear her eyes away.

"You like this?" Brynn asked, running her hands along her bra and abdomen.

"You're insanely beautiful," Kat said. "I never could've done you justice…in my fantasies."

Brynn stared into her eyes. "You're making me feel dangerous again."

"Am I?" Kat was glad she wasn't the only one so turned on. She took in shaky breaths and continued to watch, almost unable to take it all in.

"Yes, Sergeant, you are." She grinned wickedly and Kat came alive, her synapses in her brain firing once again.

"How so?"

Brynn kept moving her hands, rubbed fingertips around her sharp looking nipples. Her small breasts heaved with her quick breathing. She moaned as the sensation hit her, causing her eyes to flash.

"Tell me what to do, Kat" Brynn said, rubbing and caressing.

Kat sat up further, the sound of her name sending a shockwave straight to her heart.

"Say that again," she said. "My name. Say my name again."

"Kat," Brynn whispered.

"Yes." Kat closed her eyes. The sound of her name on the smoothest, sexiest voice she'd ever heard, was nearly earth-shattering. She wanted to hear it again and again.

"Tell me what to do, Kat. What should I do next?"

Kat opened her eyes and licked her lips, heart jumping. "Your jeans," she said. "Take them off."

Brynn slowly unbuttoned her jeans and lowered them over her hips. She peeled them off and tossed them aside just as she had the daisy. She stood before Kat in the matching panties and bra, giving her a look of pure predator. She inched closer.

"Now what?" She raised an eyebrow.

"The panties."

Brynn slipped her fingers beneath the lace and eased them off. Like her jeans, she tossed them aside.

Kat looked her up and down, felt her mouth salivating. She wanted to taste her, snake her tongue inside her folds, and take her swollen, glistening clit in her mouth and suck her off. But she held back, wanting to savor every last moment. First, she wanted to feel her.

"Come here," she said, guiding Brynn's hips so she straddled her leg. She sat up and skimmed her hands lightly up and down her sides while placing teasing kisses along her awakening skin. She smelled of earthy rain, citrus, and sandalwood. Kat couldn't help but turn her face to nibble and lick her moist skin. Brynn shuddered and she ran her hands through Kat's wet hair. She moaned softly when Kat reached the delicateness of her ribs.

"You feel good, Brynn," Kat said. "So good." She looked up at her, touching her, causing her to quiver. "I bet you're so wet."

Brynn took in a quick breath, and her eyes confirmed what Kat already knew. Kat lowered her hand and ran it carefully up her inner thigh. When she found the heat of her cunt, she slid her fingers into her slickness and moaned at the sensation.

"Kat," Brynn said quickly as she knotted her hand in Kat's hair and began slowly rocking her hips. Her eyes fell closed, and Kat stroked her, played with her full clit. Then, as Brynn rocked in her own world, Kat slid her fingers up inside.

Brynn threw her head back and called out.

"Ease down," Kat said, once again guiding her hips. Brynn, while straddling her leg, slid down onto her fingers, resting against her leg. Immediately, she began to buck.

Kat encouraged her, watching in amazement as her body moved and slithered, her beautiful eyes closing, her lips trembling. She hugged herself to Kat, jerked her hips madly.

"Fuck me," she whispered. "Oh, God yes, fuck me, Kat."

Kat kissed her chest and found her hard nipple through the lace, where she sucked and bit ever so slightly. Brynn went mad, called her name, and came in to lick Kat's ear and laugh.

Kat pulled the lace down and took her bare flesh into her mouth. She moaned as she sucked, and Brynn held fast to her head, jerking, rocking, fucking. Kat pulled away with a smack and licked up her sternum.

"Kat, Kat."

"Go ahead, baby, I've got you. Ride me."

"Oh, God it feels too good. Tell me—if I come—we'll do it again."

"Of course," Kat said. "We'll do it all night long and well into tomorrow. And then whenever you want. Over and over."

"Promise?"

"I promise."

"Oh God, I'm gonna come."

And she exploded, body arching back, pulsing. She screamed, neck straining, hair falling down her back. Kat nearly came in her pants as she held her hip and fucked her tightness, loving the way it came alive and pulsed down on her fingers. It flooded with warmth and wetness, squeezed her fingers, held on to her for life.

Brynn rocked, clung, and screamed again as she came a second time, this time softer, hoarse, throat tight and spent. She opened her eyes and moved slower, focused on Kat, and grinned. "Feels so good."

"You want to come again?"

Kat was breathless, but she was already addicted. She wanted to watch her all over again. Taste the sweat beaded on her skin. Bite on the hard nipple once again.

"Yes," Brynn said. "Please make me come again."

Kat pressed against her clit with her thumb, and Brynn bucked wildly and hugged her close, biting Kat's neck as she came in an instant, cunt throbbing and grabbing, slick and swollen. Kat held her as she shuddered against her, refusing to let go with her teeth. Kat closed her eyes so close to coming herself. She didn't dare move.

A noise sounded, a series of bells. At first, Kat didn't react, the noise off in a fog somewhere far away. But Brynn released her and spoke in her ear.

"Is that a phone?"

Kat groaned. Brynn was still wrapped around her, bearing down, pulsing with pleasure. "Sounds like it."

"Is it yours?"

"Huh?" Kat reached for her back pocket. "Yes."

"Do you need to get it?"

Kat hugged her, never wanting to let go. "No." The ringing stopped but then immediately started up again. Brynn moved. "No, wait, don't go."

Brynn held her face as she slid off of her. "You probably need to get that," she said. "Besides, I'm holding you to your promise."

She kissed her softly and then crawled on the bed and hugged a pillow, looking like a goddess waiting to be sculpted.

Kat opened and closed her sore fingers as she eyed her phone. "Shit, it's Murph." She gave Brynn an apologetic look, knowing it was something serious.

"Murph, what's up?" Kat said, answering the call.

"Kat, we've got her." He sounded excited, breathless, keyed up.

"Who?" She scratched her head and looked over at Brynn, wanting to lick the come she felt on her fingers.

"Williams. Bea Williams. You know? Hello?"

Kat shook her head. "What?"

"Wallace is bringing her in right now."

The realization sunk in, and she panicked and worried for Brynn. "Is she—okay?" She glanced back at Brynn who suddenly looked concerned.

"Who? Williams?" He sounded incredulous. "She's scuffed up, but Wallace is worse off. She fought hard."

Kat didn't speak, just closed her eyes. "I'll be right there."

"Thought you'd want to know."

"Thanks."

She ended the call, sighed, and ran a hand through her hair.

"Is she okay?" Brynn asked, sitting up.

"She's uh…being brought in now. She fought."

Brynn crawled from the bed. "I'm going with you."

Kat hadn't necessarily wanted to go, but she knew Brynn would insist. "You can't. There's not anything you can do."

Brynn grabbed her clothes and began dressing. "There's always a way to help someone. And this is my sister, so don't even try and stop me."

Kat watched her. Saw her determination and the red rising from her chest up to her face. She was upset and worried. But most of all, she was scared. She tried to hide it, but Kat could see it now. She could finally read her. But was it too little too late?

CHAPTER THIRTEEN

The car ride back from Charlottetown was heavy with silence. Brynn kept her eyes trained forward, afraid to look at Kat. The scent of her tantalizing cologne was all over her, and she fought closing her eyes and reliving what they'd just shared. But if she did, she'd lose it. Control, emotions, fear, all of it. She had to stay focused on Bea. Had to help her somehow. Would Kat help? Could she count on her? With a slap, she was again reminded of how different they were. Kat was a cop, her responsibility the law. She had a responsibility to protect Bea. Again, she wanted to look over, but she fought it and stared straight ahead, despite feeling Kat's gaze skimming her every so often.

"Are you okay?" Kat finally asked.

Brynn's skin came alive and heated with the sound of her voice. She recalled the feel of her strong shoulders and neck beneath her hands as she'd held on to her for dear life. The feel of those long, glorious fingers up inside her working magic. Brynn cleared her throat.

"I'm not sure."

Kat drove on, and the thick wall of silence between them reformed. Brynn could barely breathe it was so stifling. Worry finally won out and she spoke.

"Is she hurt?"

Kat sighed, as if she didn't want to tell her. "Murph said she was scuffed up."

"Oh God." Brynn rested her head on her hand as she leaned against the door. "Great."

"I guess Wallace, the one who arrested her, I guess he got the worst of it."

Brynn took in a sharp breath. "God damn it, Bea. They'll hold that against her, won't they?"

Kat blinked a few times quickly as if she couldn't believe the question. "Yes." She shook her head. "She resisted arrest and assaulted an officer. We don't take that lightly."

"What if she was high and not in her right mind?"

Kat flexed her jaw, and Brynn knew she sounded desperate, irrational. But she couldn't help herself, she was grasping at straws. Bea couldn't go to jail. It would be her ultimate failure as a guardian. Not to mention the danger her sister would be put in on a daily basis. She knew that threat firsthand and had spent quite a bit of time in isolation because of it. Isolation had saved her life and kept trouble from finding her.

"She won't survive prison," Brynn said. "She just won't." Her bravado, her mouth, her bad attitude, she'd be toast. Brynn stared out the windshield at the waning lights of mostly countryside. People were in their homes, watching television, reading a good book, oblivious to pending charges or jail or a prison sentence. She longed to be one of them. Just for a night. Just for a minute. Long enough to close her eyes and take a deep breath.

"Try not to worry," Kat said. "Your sister's tough. Hold on to that."

Brynn wanted to argue but couldn't. Kat was right. Bea was tough. She was hard as a rock and stubborn. She used to wonder if Bea ever felt fear. Or ever had feelings of concern for anyone else. She knew the answer was probably no, but she couldn't imagine that when those feelings were so strong in herself. Her eyes drifted closed despite her racing heart. The strain of the night was catching up to her. Stress always caused a fight-or-flight reaction in her, and then she'd crash, completely drained.

She forced her eyes open and stared in a daze out the window. When Kat finally pulled into the station, she had to blink to regain reality. A tightness in her chest returned as they entered the building. She recalled the first night she'd been brought in by Kat herself. She'd been terrified yet de-termined and she'd refused to speak, not even to Kat who had tried to comfort her a little. For an arresting officer, she'd been polite, respectful. And Brynn soon had learned that none of them believed their story. They had known Bea was guilty, but Brynn wouldn't own up to it. So they'd had no choice but to solely charge Brynn.

"I don't like this place," Brynn said. Kat waved at an officer working the front desk, and he buzzed a door that let them in. They wound through the station and Brynn wiped sweaty palms on her jeans.

Kat brought her to where she'd been questioned before and offered her a seat against the wall. Then she disappeared. Around her, uniformed officers came and went, and one even offered to get her a coffee. She declined and waited for what felt like hours. Then Kat appeared looking grim. "Would you like to see her?"

Brynn followed her into the tiny interrogation room she'd been in before. Bea was sitting at the table, eyes wide, chewing on the skin around her nails. She stood when they entered.

"Brynn."

"Are you okay?" They settled back down at the table, and Bea's eyes shifted to Kat who took the hint.

"You've got ten minutes, then she needs to go to holding," Kat said softly.

Brynn nodded. She wanted to hold her hands but didn't take the chance that they were allowed. And whether she wanted to admit it or not, Bea most likely wouldn't want to. She'd never been an affectionate person. Not even when it was for comfort.

"Are you hurt?" She scanned her for bruises, but all she could see were superficial scrapes, mussed hair, and smeared eyeliner. Her sweatshirt was filthy and her nails were long and dirty. She needed a bath, a good scrub. And by the hollows in her cheeks, a good meal.

She shook her head. "I'm fine."

"Where have you been?"

"Around." She motioned toward the mirror.

Brynn looked back. "You should tell them everything, Bea. It could help you get a lighter—"

"I'm no rat," she said. She stared into the mirror with a hard set to her jaw.

Brynn sighed. "What are you being charged with?"

Bea rolled her eyes. "A lot. But they're dropping some of it because of what we did for Sergeant Vander and her partner. I guess he's doing better so that helps."

"Bea, you have to give them more. Something they can use so you won't go to jail. This is your life."

"I won't, Brynn. I can't. Can't you do something? Say something?" She looked desperate, like a wild-eyed animal caught in a trap.

"Like what?"

"I don't know. Tell them you told me to run. Tell them that I'm an addict. That I can't help myself."

"They can hear everything we're saying, Bea."

She sat back and banged her hand on the table. "Then fuck this. And fuck them."

Brynn shook her head, desperately trying to reach her. "Bea, it's all up to you this time. I'll say what I can, but this time it is solely on you."

Bea chewed off the tip of a fingernail and spit. Her eyes narrowed. "That cop, the one who arrested me, he scared me. It was self-defense. And the heroin…"

"Drugs? You got caught with drugs?"

Bea scoffed and looked away.

"Bea?"

"Don't start, Brynn." She started in on another nail, spit it across the room, and then shoved the sleeves up on her sweatshirt. Brynn recoiled at the sight of bruised inner elbows and various needle marks.

"Oh, Jesus." Brynn felt dizzy, nauseous. Who was this woman sitting across from her? They couldn't possibly be blood related. Bea couldn't possibly have been raised by her.

"What?" Bea glanced at her own arms and then grinned. "This bother you? You always were the chicken shit."

"Bea, why?" She wanted to plead with her, grab her and shake her, fall to her feet and cry.

"Why not? I mean, you really ought to get that stick out of your ass and have a little fun, Brynn. You have no idea how good it feels."

Brynn felt her own jaw tighten and rage began to boil her blood. "I guess I've been too busy taking care of your ass, going to prison for you, protecting you, feeding you, clothing you, keeping a roof over your head. I guess I've been too busy making sure you survive to worry about having fun with drugs."

Bea stared at her with steely eyes. "That supposed to make me feel guilty or something?" She rolled her eyes.

Brynn had had enough. Tears gnawed at her throat and she was so angry she wanted to flip the table. Instead, she stood. "No. I don't expect you to feel anything. Not anymore."

She stepped to the door, heard a buzz, and then saw Kat pull it open.

"You okay?" Kat whispered.

Bea laughed. "Oh, so this is classic. You desert me and you're all cozy with the cop? Beautiful, Brynn. Beautiful."

"Enjoy prison, Bea." She studied her long and hard. Bea would get beaten at first, yes, but then, honestly, she'd fit right in. Probably even help run the drugs. She belonged there, and Brynn had to finally accept it. "Somehow I know you will." She walked through the door past Kat and headed for the front where she'd come in. Behind her, she heard Bea yelling at her as she was being walked to holding. But Brynn didn't turn around. She was done. She was finally and completely done. Tears racked her body, but she swallowed them down and wiped her eyes. She refused to cry. Not anymore, not for Bea.

She stopped at the door where the officer had buzzed her in. She breathed deeply.

Someone touched her shoulder from behind. Brynn turned and found Kat looking at her with the most understanding look she'd ever seen. She fell into her arms.

"I'll speak to the D.A," she said, holding her tightly.

Brynn shuddered as she battled her tears. "No, don't. She gets what she gets."

Kat pulled away. "You don't mean that."

"I do. I'm done, Kat. I'm done. She belongs in prison."

Kat held her again. "Come on, let's get you home."

Brynn pushed away and wiped her face. "No, I need to be alone. I just want to be alone."

"But, Brynn, it's the middle of the night."

She left Kat standing as she walked through first one door and then the other, out into the humid night. She crossed the slick street and headed for the overgrown grassy shoulder. She need to walk, to cry, to think. And she needed to do it all on her own.

CHAPTER FOURTEEN

K at turned and sighed, fed up with trying to sleep. It was four forty-five, early morning. She sat up and slipped into clothes. Gunner jumped down and followed her into the kitchen. She switched on a low light and started the coffee. Her mind was still going ninety miles an hour, just as it had since the last time she'd seen Brynn walking out the door of the police station. She tried to ignore it, to push it away by going through the motions of a morning routine. But Brynn held fast in her mind, and Kat couldn't take it much more.

It had been weeks since she'd spoken to her. She'd left messages, driven by. Brynn had responded to none of it. Rumor was, Brynn was planning on moving away, going back to school, starting over. But her family was fighting it, somehow keeping her entangled in the drama on Williams Lane. Each time Kat had driven down the dirt drive, various members of the Williams family would surface out of dark spaces and meander over to the car. They never spoke, just walked slowly with hard looks like zombies hell-bent on cornering dinner. It freaked her out enough to stay in her vehicle, and her desperate glances at Brynn's house produced nothing but Billy Williams glaring at her from the porch.

If she could just see her and speak to her, share her own good news, Brynn would cheer up, she was sure of it. She sipped her coffee and scratched Gunner's head. She'd been pretty low-key about her career change and possibly moving to the CID or Criminal Investigations Division. Though she was excited and thrilled, something else had come up, something she hadn't expected. Another precinct wanted her, offered her a similar position in the city. At first, she'd thought about turning them down right away, but the more she thought about it, the more promising it seemed. Damien would never be able to return to work. His injuries were too severe, and he was having to learn how to do almost everything all over again. The good news was he was in good spirits and one hell of a fighter. He even had her betting with him on when he would be able to do what.

Kat glanced out the window and saw daybreak. Gunner wagged his tail as if anticipating. She sipped her coffee and smiled at him, causing him to bark. He stood and danced, lifting one excited paw after another.

"All right, boy, we'll go." She left the coffee and opened the door to the basement. Gunner descended like a mad man. She followed carefully and walked to her workbench. There, she changed into a bikini and surf shorts and tugged on her thin racing life jacket. Next, she fastened Gunner's life jacket around him and opened the back door. He took off across the yard and out onto the deck. He barked at the Sea-Doo tied to the dock. Kat grabbed her backpack full of gear and snacks and slung it on.

She closed the door behind her and walked onto the dock. Carefully, she stepped on her Sea-Doo, put down a towel for Gunner, and straddled the seat. Then she softly called Gunner who hesitantly stepped down in front of her. She lifted him into position and he settled and barked with excitement. She untied the watercraft from the dock, removed the key from her wristband, and started the engine. They took off, slowly at first and then faster and faster until the Sea-Doo was wide open, flying across the water. She smiled into the wind and mist. Gunner panted, ears back. She rode until she came to their special cove where she pulled in and killed the engine. She tied off on a tree stretching into the water, and she and Gunner waded onto the shore.

They sat and ate beef jerky and stared out onto the water. A distant fisherman in his bass boat sat slumped in his tall chair. Kat shivered a little as the cool mountain water evaporated from her skin. She sat back and closed her eyes, wondering again if she could ever leave this town, this lake… Brynn. If she did, one thing was for certain, she'd have to have closure, she'd have to say good-bye.

❖

Kat ran her hand through her hair and pulled into Williams Lane. She was freshly showered and dressed nicely for Damien's welcome home party. And she was on a mission to find Brynn Williams. Damien and his wife were insisting Brynn come, and they had made it Kat's responsibility to talk her into it. Kat hadn't exactly argued about it, secretly excited at having a reason to go and find her.

People looked out their windows and some stepped out onto their porch to eye the stranger in the small SUV driving down their lane. She waved but knew it was useless. The stares were not friendly. Regardless, she pulled into Brynn's gravel drive and stared at the front porch. With a deep breath, she climbed from the car and hurried to the front door. Behind her, she saw the zombies emerge from their dark spaces and head toward her. There were four of them and they looked more than pissed. They looked deadly. One carried a shotgun.

The door opened. Brynn looked just as shocked as she felt. "Kat."

"Brynn, hi. Can I come inside?" She looked back; the zombies loomed.

Brynn pushed hair away from her face. "Uh, I don't think that's a good idea."

"Please? I need to talk to you."

Brynn pushed open the worn screen and stepped onto the porch. She waved the zombies off, but they didn't stop.

"Friends of yours?" Kat said with a nervous laugh. She tried not to stare at Brynn in cutoff jeans and a threadbare gray tank top. She'd been in the sun and her skin seemed to glow.

"My uncle," she said. "And his boys."

"Oh, well, they look…friendly enough."

"They'd eat your heart if they could."

Kat laughed nervously until she saw the serious look on Brynn's face.

"Can we go inside then? Talk?"

Brynn sighed. "You shouldn't be here."

"Why? I mean why do they hate me so much?"

Brynn smiled. "Because you put me away, Sergeant. Don't you remember? And your people put Bea away."

Kat felt herself heat. "It's not exactly like that," she said.

"I know that. But they don't. And they refuse to listen to me when I tell them otherwise." They both stared back at the approaching men. "Don't feel too bad. They just hate the law. It's not specific to you."

"Oh, well, that's nice to know."

"They're very territorial," Brynn said, staring ahead. "Don't fuck with them."

"I don't plan on it."

Brynn opened the screen door. "You better get inside then." Kat hurried inside and stopped in the dim light. The house was frigid cold and smelled of cigarettes. Light tried to come through closed blinds, but it wasn't enough for her to step confidently.

"This way." Brynn walked through what Kat suspected was the living room. A man, one she assumed to be Billy, was asleep on the couch, the old television tuned in to cartoons.

Brynn crossed to the kitchen and sat at a table, the sunlight streaming in strong in this room, so strongly Kat had to cover her brow and squint until she adjusted.

"What do you need to talk about?" Brynn sipped what looked like Sun Drop from a sweaty glass.

Kat settled in across from her and took in the framed photos of Brynn's family along the dining room wall.

"It's Damien. He's coming home today, and he wants you to be there with him to celebrate."

Brynn laughed and traced the sweat on her glass. "He said that?"

"He did."

Brynn met her eyes. "I seriously doubt he cares if I'm there or not."

"You're wrong," Kat whispered. "He wants you there. We all want you there."

Brynn looked away but not before Kat saw her pulse jump in her neck.

"I've missed you," she said. "I've wanted nothing more than to know how you are. Talk to you...hold you."

Brynn stood. "You can't talk like that here." She took her glass and dumped it in the sink. Stood in front of it, in front of the window, glowing like a goddess. Kat was breathless with desire, but it was obvious Brynn was terrified.

"Come with me to the party," Kat said. "So we can have fun and talk some."

"You really want a Williams girl at this party?" She was scowling, arms folded across her chest.

Kat walked to her. "You're Brynn. Not Bea or Billy or those men out there. You're Brynn and I see you. I see who you really are." Brynn inhaled sharply; she trembled. Kat touched her, ran her hands up the outside of her arms. "Come here." She enveloped her and drew in the scent of her hair and moist skin. Both went straight to her spine like a bolt of lightning. She, too, shuddered.

"What in the hell is this?" a voice said from behind. Brynn cried out and pushed Kat away. She turned toward the refrigerator as if she were afraid to look at him.

The older man Kat had seen outside stood with his shotgun hanging down his leg. His overalls were filthy and so were his hands. He'd been working with soil; she could smell it. Probably his garden.

"She was just leaving," Brynn said.

"You're that cop, ain't ya?" He looked at Kat with pure disgust.

"I just came to check on Brynn."

He jerked his chin toward Brynn. "She's fine. See? She don't need you checking in on her."

Kat held up her hands. "I see that, thank you." She looked to Brynn. "Think about it," she said. "He'd love to see you. We all would."

Kat excused herself and edged past the angry uncle. She recognized him from his lengthy rap sheet. Mostly DUIs, breaking and entering. Mo, his name was Mo. Short for Montgomery. She hurried outside and found his boys meandering around her car. Her heart raced as she unlocked the door and climbed in. She started the engine, but the boys didn't move. She edged down her window. "You want me gone, then let me go."

They moved but continued their dead-eyed stare. Kat sped off, kicking up dirt. But just before she turned onto the main road, she saw Brynn emerge and stare off after her, wiping tears from her eyes.

Chapter Fifteen

Brynn could hear the music as she walked up the sidewalk past all the cars edged to the curb. Balloons sprouted from the front porch lights, and laughter spilled out into the brick entryway. She rang the doorbell and did last-minute adjustments of her hair and clothes. The outfit was new; one she'd bought when she'd taken Billy shopping. Her pants were linen, ivory in color, and they matched her linen button-up shirt which she wore open over a white silk tank. She looked very relaxed but well put together.

The door angled open, and Damien's wife, Genie, beamed, hand to throat in a gesture of disbelief.

"Brynn, oh my Lord, get in here." She embraced her, and Brynn stood in shock at the sudden show of affection. "We didn't think you were coming."

They pulled apart, and Brynn handed over the wine she'd stopped and bought. It wasn't expensive, but it wasn't eight-dollar wine either.

"Oh, you didn't have to do this." She took her hand and led her inside. "Damien's in the back with the boys at the grill."

Brynn scanned quickly but didn't see Kat anywhere. Her heart sank, yet her stomach still did flips. Genie uncorked the wine to let it breathe, but Brynn approached the counter and slid her a nearby glass. "If you don't mind, I think I'll take some of that now."

She smiled and studied her as she poured. "Kat's not here yet."

"Hmm?" Brynn sipped her wine, still staring out to the backyard.

"Kat, she got a call. They found the guys from the SUV."

Brynn nearly dropped her glass. "Is she okay? I mean—"

"She's fine. She wasn't on duty when they found them."

Brynn released a long-held breath. She closed her eyes and hugged herself with one arm. She downed the rest of her wine.

"Come," Genie said. "Sit." She refilled her wineglass and left the bottle on the coffee table. Then she relaxed and crossed her legs. She smiled softly, sincerely. "You know we've known Kat a very long time."

Brynn lifted her brow. "Oh?"

"Almost ten years. And in all that time I've never seen her quite like she is now."

Brynn knew she was supposed to ask what she meant, but she knew what she was getting at. Instead she drank her wine and watched as Damien's friends drank and laughed, patting him on the shoulders as he sat in his wheelchair.

"Your home is very nice," Brynn said, looking around. She loved the vaulted ceilings, the raw wood floors, the large stone fireplace.

Genie didn't respond. Just stared at her. "How long have you been in love with Kat?"

Brynn nearly spit out her wine. "I'm sorry?"

"How long? I'm guessing it was pretty much right away on your part. You're more emotional than our Kat, passionate. Probably a romantic?"

Brynn couldn't speak. She set down her glass. It shook in her hand. "I, uh, maybe I should go?"

"Oh, I'm sorry. You aren't out are you? No wonder why you look so scared."

Brynn stood, heart racing. It had taken everything she had to sneak off up to May's, change clothes, and take off in her car. She had said she was going to a party and May hadn't asked much more. Uncle Mo had stared after her as she'd driven off. He hadn't liked Kat being at the house, hadn't liked their embrace. He'd questioned her, stared into her bones and melted them. He knew something was up; he could smell it. He had told her to tell Kat not to come back. If she did he would consider it trespassing.

Brynn had gone to her room and slammed things around, so tired of being under the eye of her family. They, of course, were blaming her for Bea's incarceration. Said she should've done more. They no longer trusted her, and rumors about her growing friendship with Kat and Damien had apparently made its way to Williams Lane. Her family watched her from a distance, from right next door, sometimes from the kitchen table. Uncle Mo had made himself more than comfortable one morning before she awoke to find him sitting there smoking a cigarette. "Your lady cop friend drove by again." He'd blown smoke out his nose and narrowed his eyes. "What does she want, Brynn?"

Brynn shook her head, pushing his face away from the center of her mind. He was dangerous, and she shouldn't be here and definitely should not be having this conversation.

"Don't leave." Genie came to her side and gently clasped her hand. "I didn't mean to scare you off." She brushed her face with smooth knuckles. "You're safe here. We know about Kat. We love her and we're growing to love you too."

"I can't...I shouldn't be here." Her voice caved with nerves.

"Kat's coming back. She called not long ago...wondering if you were here."

Brynn looked at the door. If she left what would she do? Go home, watch another rerun with Billy? Answer more of

Mo's questions when he demanded answers? Go through to-morrow just like today, cleaning and working in the garden? Staring off into space dreaming of Kat and a life she could've had in a different universe?

No. She was fed up. She deserved a life just like anyone else did.

She nodded and Genie led her back to the couch. "I take it your family doesn't know?"

Brynn swallowed hard. "No."

"Are you afraid to tell them?"

Brynn laughed. "Yes, terrified." She stared at her hands. "Although I think my uncle suspects something."

"What would he do?"

"Uncle Mo? Oh, I don't know. I know he loves me, but he's very alpha male and he's protective. If he thinks something's not right or something's hurting me, there's no telling what he'd do."

"And he would think this…Kat…would be wrong?"

"I'm afraid so."

Brynn heard the door open behind her, and Genie stood and welcomed more people. Brynn made her way outside, kissed Damien, took the beer he offered, and nearly downed it at once. She needed to relax, and she willed the buzz to come on and soften the edges. She smiled as other police men and women shook her hand, thanking her for brave actions. She nodded politely, felt herself blush, and tried to be friendly. But honestly, she still felt like she could've done more for Damien. But his smile and toast to her said he obviously didn't think so. She took another offered beer and fell into conversation with the department psychologist. They were discussing her schooling for counseling when Damien threw his hands up and shouted.

"Vander, get your ass over here!"

Brynn turned and saw Kat standing on the back patio, beer in hand. She smiled at Damien and held up her beer. "We got 'em!"

The backyard erupted in cheer. Kat got so many hugs and back slaps, Brynn wasn't sure how she remained standing upright. Brynn stood where she was, not wanting to intrude. This crowd deserved a celebration, and she wasn't about to interfere. She sipped her beer and watched Kat with her friends and colleagues. Her smile was incredible, her mood contagious. And when she laughed, Brynn's heart fluttered. Two people stepped into her view, and Brynn quietly moved, smiled, and nodded at another friendly face and then stopped and refocused on Kat. She couldn't take her eyes off her. She'd changed her shirt from when she'd last seen her. The new tight white tee, deep v-neck shirt showed off a sliver of a red tattoo. From where she stood it looked like it could be a heart. She wondered who it was for. Jealousy burned through her, and she tried to shove it away, drinking more. She turned, pissed that the sight of the tattoo on Kat's muscular chest turned her on a little. What else didn't she know about her? She was one hell of a good lover; she knew that much.

"Excuse me," a familiar voice said from behind.

Brynn stilled, the tenor of the voice, like a gentle breath kissing the back of her neck. She knew it was Kat. Knew she was standing there looking gorgeous in the tee and worn jeans and boots.

"Yes?" Brynn said, turning.

Kat pointed to the ground. "You dropped your smile."

Brynn closed her eyes, so moved by the blue of Kat's eyes. She shook with laughter, unable not to. "That's the worst pickup line I've ever heard."

She heard Kat laugh. "Oh, come on. It's good. And it's true. You were smiling just a moment ago. What happened?"

Brynn opened her eyes and her gaze took in all of Kat. Her tight blond ponytail, the tan of her skin, the muscles of her neck, shoulders, and chest. The tattoo. She blinked as she tried to look away from it.

Kat caught her looking. She tugged on her shirt. "You don't like it?"

Brynn stared at the full red heart. An arrow was running through it, and a drop of red dripped from the bottom point.

"There's no name," Brynn said before she realized it.

Kat smiled. "No, not yet. I wanted to ask her permission first."

"Oh." Brynn looked away. She suddenly felt dizzy, a little wobbly. She could smell Kat's cologne from where she stood, and it was awakening every cell in her body and causing them all to heat, adding to the dizziness. She had to get away or she would throw herself in her arms and beg her to take her home and have her way with her. But this was not the time or place, and who's to say the heart was for her? But the mere idea that it might be…dear God, it moved her.

"Would you excuse me, please?" She moved toward the patio and deposited her beer on a table nearby. She heard Kat call after her, but she kept moving. Faces smiled and blurred. Voices laughed and carried. All of it morphed around her as she moved. She entered the house and went straight for the front door. Kat caught her just as she reached for the door handle. Brynn breathed rapidly as she stared at Kat's strong hand over hers.

"Wait, please," Kat said.

Brynn straightened. "I really have to go."

"Tell me why," she said softly.

Brynn trembled. She panicked. She nearly fainted. And then she came back, refocused and weighted with determination. "Because I'm in love with you."

Silence.

Kat slowly removed her hand from hers. Then, gently, it was placed on her shoulder. Brynn turned and found Kat's eyes searching hers madly. Heat kissed her cheeks.

"What did you say?" she whispered. She blinked quickly, the way she did when she was in disbelief.

"I said," Brynn said, voice trembling, "that I'm in love with you."

Kat inhaled and then grabbed her by the arms. "You have no idea what that just did to me do you?"

Brynn's dizziness intensified. "I have a pretty good idea."

Kat looked around, then glanced at the door. "Want to get out of here?"

Brynn sighed. "More than anything."

Kat opened the door and led her out with her hand on the small of her back. They hurried down the brick walkway, beyond the buoyant balloons, and out onto the street. The sun had just set and the streetlights were winking to life. Kat reached for her hand and Brynn took it, warming inside. She felt good, safe. And then with a glimpse of approaching men, it all came crashing down.

She stopped, frozen.

Mo and his sons walked up slowly, meeting them head on in the street. They didn't appear to have weapons, but that did little to control Brynn's sudden panic.

"What are you doing here?" she asked hurriedly, releasing Kat's hand. But Kat grabbed hers again and held tightly. A quick glance at her showed a stern flexing jaw, heat on her cheeks, and a determined flash to her eyes. "Mo?" Brynn was desperate to quell the situation, whatever the situation was. Kat was about to blow and that would be bad, very bad.

Mo held Kat's stare. He shoved his hands in his pockets and shrugged. "We came to see what this party is all about."

Brynn again tried to release from Kat, but Kat wouldn't let her. "Mo, this is a party for Deputy Damien. You know, Sergeant Vander's partner who was shot?"

He smiled. "Yeah, I know who he is." He tugged on his Red Man tobacco ball cap and rubbed the scruff of his growing beard. He'd cleaned up since their encounter at the house, and he and his sons stood in jeans, worn cowboy boots, and T-shirts. She couldn't help but notice that Kat wore it so much better.

"Question is," Mo said, finally looking at Brynn. "What are you doing here? And why in the hell are you holding her hand?" He turned slightly and spit. Her cousin Marty laughed. He was always a little shit, picking on Billy, taking advantage of him.

She glared at him. "Don't you have barns to go break into and steal from?"

He stopped laughing. "Least I ain't no queer."

Heat exploded inside her, and she clenched her fist and took a step forward. "No, you prefer your right hand. God knows you can't get anyone else to touch you."

He squared off with her, wad of chew in his jaw. His eyes, hazel green like hers, were beady and sinister. "Watch yourself, cousin. If you weren't kin..."

"What? You'd hit me? Nice." She looked at Mo. "You must be so proud."

Kat squeezed her hand and turned as a few of her colleagues approached from behind.

"Everything okay, Vander?"

"It will be as soon as these fellas turn tail and leave."

Mo scoffed. "What? Ain't ya'll gonna invite us in?"

"We'll treat you just like you treat us. So what do you think?"

He looked at his boys and laughed. Then he looked at Brynn. "We just came for what's ours. Brynny, let's go."

She closed her eyes and stepped back and touched Kat's arm with her free hand in an obvious embrace. "No."

He reared back in obvious disbelief. "What?"

"I said no. I'm staying. These are my friends. I'm allowed friends."

"Not when they're the law you're not."

"It shouldn't matter who they are."

He shook his head. "We ain't like these people," he said. "And we don't need the law around." He tugged on his cap again in frustration. "Now come on. Billy's waiting for you."

"Billy's fine." He was working, doing his daily ritual. He was doing well. He no longer needed her all the time. It was as hard for her to admit that to herself as it was to admit it to Mo.

"Brynny, I ain't playin' here."

"She isn't either," Kat said. "You heard her answer."

He glanced at their enclosed hands. "Brynny, it's us or them. You choose. Right here, right now."

"No."

He raised an eyebrow.

"I shouldn't have to choose between those I care about, and I won't. I love my family and I love my new friends."

"You can't have us and have them," he said.

"Just watch me."

"Don't come home," he said. "Ever again."

"I'll come home when I damn well please. That house is in my name and so is the lot. Billy's my brother, and I'll care for him. Unless…you want to take him on? Pay for his food and clothes, care for his needs?"

Mo looked away and she knew she had him. "Have a nice night, Uncle Mo. I'll be home tomorrow."

She turned and pulled on Kat. The surrounding cops squeezed her arm and shoulder as they moved through them.

Brynn shook from the confrontation, and when they were enclosed with friends, she fell into Kat and held her tight. Tears threatened, but she fought them, concentrating instead on Kat's heartbeat.

When she finally pulled away and nodded to everyone that she was okay, she looked back down the road to find Mo and her cousins gone.

And for the first time in her entire life, she felt free.

CHAPTER SIXTEEN

Kat turned on two lamps in the living room, keeping the room low lit with a warm glow. She lit a candle on the coffee table and lit a dozen tea light candles along her dresser in the bedroom. She fumbled with her iPod and put on Aoife O'Donovan. Then she stood at the door next to Gunner and waited for the old Lincoln to pull in her drive. The old Lincoln that carried the woman she could not stop thinking about. The woman who turned her on, lit her up from the inside, made her insides flutter and turn to mush. The woman, she now realized, she loved.

The old Lincoln's headlights flashed in her eyes as it pulled into the driveway. Gunner barked and wagged his tail. She touched his head and grew nervous, surprising herself. After all this time, Brynn still made her nervous. She got so caught up in her looks, her scent, the thought of touching her, it all swirled around inside leaving her feeling clumsy and antsy. But despite all of those feelings and the craziness, she smiled as Brynn walked to the door, buttoned-down outer shirt gone, leaving the lone white tank and linen pants.

Kat forced herself to wait for a knock before she opened the door. Brynn smiled at her shyly and Kat's heart sang, and she suddenly had so much she wanted to say and do. She took her hand and pulled her inside, closing the door and tugging her close. She held her hips and stared into her eyes, brimming with tears.

"My God, I love you," Kat said. She closed her eyes and kissed her so softly, gently, just enough to taste her, feel her. Brynn's hands found her shoulders and neck as she returned the kiss just as gently and softly. Kat spoke between kisses. "I've been waiting by that door for ten minutes, but I've just realized, I've been waiting for you for a lifetime."

Brynn tugged her closer, kissed her harder, capturing Kat's lips with her own. "I know what you mean," she whispered. "Who would've thought you've been here all along."

"Just down the road."

"In a sexy cop outfit."

Kat laughed. "Oh, how you hated me."

Brynn lightly kissed her neck. "I didn't hate you. I hated my situation."

"You went to prison for her, didn't you?"

"Yeah."

Kat tilted her chin. "Who does that? You really are amazing."

A tear slipped down Brynn's cheek. "When I love...I love deeply...for life."

"Lucky me," Kat said, touching her face. She kissed her tear. Brynn tugged the ponytail holder from Kat's hair and tossed it aside. Her eyes widened as she ran her hands through Kat's hair.

"No, lucky me." She smiled.

Kat stroked her cheek, searching her eyes. "You've had a very big evening."

"Mm."

"How do you feel?" She needed to make sure she was okay. Her eyes looked tired but strong, full of color and sparkle. But the brimming tears told of something more.

"Happy." She closed her eyes. "Free. Free to be me." She opened her eyes and took Kat in. "But mostly free to love."

Kat kissed her, softly at first, then more hungrily, determined. Brynn returned the kiss with vigor, sneaking out her tongue to tease and taste, causing Kat to moan with delight. Kat caught her tongue with her lips a few times, and other times she met it with her own. It was a beautiful, slick dance and duel with playful tongues.

She pulled away and Brynn nibbled her neck, causing a shockwave to shoot up her spine.

"I seem to remember something about a promise..."

Brynn laughed and blushed.

"Is that a blush?"

"I tend to get carried away."

"Well, here's to getting carried away," Kat said as she lifted her and twirled. Brynn laughed and blushed harder.

Kat stopped and held her face. "Are you going to be shy now?"

"I don't know. It's different now. Real. You have my heart. I can't explain how deeply I feel."

Kat leaned in and brushed her hair from her ear. "Then show me."

Brynn stared into her and nodded. She took her hand and led her through the living room to the bedroom. She turned as she entered, smiling softly. "Nice," she said, referring to the candles. She backed in, pulling Kat with her. Gunner settled outside the door. Brynn placed a palm on Kat's chest, covering her tattoo. Then she leaned in and kissed her own hand, then moved it and delicately kissed the tattoo.

"I saw this from a distance and I got so turned on."

Kat held her head, warm auburn hair spilling over her hand. "Really? I didn't think you liked it."

"Oh, I liked it. I just wondered who it was for."

Kat kissed her head. "It's for you, silly woman."

Brynn kissed it again and ran her tongue around the edge, tugging her shirt aside to do so. Then she nibbled and kissed firmly and sucked. "Is there any doubt now how I feel about it?"

Kat shuddered as she moved closer to her breast. "No. No doubt."

"Good."

She lowered her hands and lifted Kat's shirt over her head. Then she lightly kissed her chest and shoulders as she reached around and unfastened her bra, letting it fall to the floor. She teased Kat's hardening nipples with her breath, and she went lower and unfastened her jeans, tugging them down and off.

She stepped back and ate Kat alive with her eyes. When she finally looked up at her, she looked like a wolf honing in on prey. She stepped closer, then reached out and was just about to touch her, when she dropped her hands.

"Now undress me," she said.

She was breathing as hard as Kat as she watched Kat step in and carefully remove her tank top. She sighed and turned her head to the side and whispered, "Not yet," when Kat ran her hands up her side. "Not quite yet." She took Kat's hands and kissed them and then placed them on her bra. "Keep going," she said. "Undress me."

Kat's hands trembled as she unfastened her bra and let it fall from her fingers. Then, trying her best not to touch her, she slid the linen pants down and away from her, leaving only her panties. "More lace," Kat said.

"Mm, I dressed with someone in mind."

Kat grinned, hooked her fingertips into the panties, and tugged downward. Brynn stepped out of them carefully and stood before her, flickering in the candlelight.

They stared into one another, chests heaving, nipples awakening, bodies quivering. "I want you to look at me," Brynn said. "Look at all the places you want to touch me."

Kat let her eyes drift down her body to her taut breasts, tight abdomen, and angled hips. She stared at her trimmed pussy, auburn curls nestled above her fold. She could see the glistening of her arousal on her smooth lips.

"Is that where you want to touch me most?"

Kat nodded.

"Me too," Brynn breathed. "I've been dying to feel your wet pussy."

Kat heated at the words, and Brynn came to her, gently wrapping her fingers around her wrist.

"I want you to touch me. Touch me while I touch you."

Kat reached out. Brynn released her. They found each other at the same time, warm fingers into hot folds. Both jerked and sighed as fingers slipped and slid against aching flesh. Kat went up to tiptoes when Brynn found her clit and framed it, stroking the length of it. She did the same back, and Brynn tossed her head back and bucked.

"Mm, am I hot?" she asked.

Kat fought closing her eyes at the sensation beneath her fingers and between her legs. "Yes. God yes."

"Wet?"

"Uh-huh. Very."

"You want to get hotter, wetter?" She stroked her quicker, faster, then slowed, squeezed her fingers, and pulled, milking her clit. Kat fought to stay upright and not collapse to her knees.

"Is that possible?"

"Oh, anything is possible," Brynn said. She continued to tug on her, and Kat felt another rush of arousal flood her cunt. Brynn groaned and went lower, swirled around her hole and then stroked the length of her as she came back up with new slickness coating her magical fingers. "See?" She moved closer and used all four fingers to smother her and circle her flesh, again and again.

Kat quivered, knees threatening to buckle. She couldn't move, couldn't breathe. But Brynn insisted, slowing. "Touch me like this," she said.

Kat tried, but she was so close to coming all over her hand. "I-I can't."

"Yes, you can." She slowed even more and released some of the pressure, stroking her lightly. The change took her breath away, and Kat had to blink away the floating stars she saw. She straightened, struggled for breath, and refocused on Brynn who looked so deliciously devilish.

"You love this don't you?"

Brynn looked at her with hooded eyes. The corner of her mouth lifted. "I like playing with you, yes."

"What if I made you stop? What if I took control?"

Brynn grinned fully. "You won't. Not yet." She increased the pressure again and circled her hand, pressing and sliding. Kat whipped back, grabbing her wrist. "Jesus."

"Now, touch me like this."

Kat did so, circling her hand in a similar manner, making sure to coat her fingers in Brynn's hot liquid. Brynn jerked, clenched her teeth, and groaned. "That's it. Yes."

They played with each other, toyed, jerked, and cried out. And just when Kat was about to break and surge over the falls in orgasm, Brynn stopped and Kat nearly collapsed.

"On the bed," she said. "Now."

Kat crawled up on the bed with her and they met in the middle, both on their knees. Brynn kissed her hard, pushing and insisting with her tongue. Then she did the same with her fingers, pushing them up deep inside Kat, causing her to call out and then whimper with uncontrollable pleasure. She looked into Brynn's eyes and knew what she wanted. Kissing her back, plunging with her own tongue, she slid her fingers up inside Brynn and fucked her long and slow just as she was being fucked. Their hips jerked and bucked, their breaths becoming pants of ecstasy. Soon Brynn began to fuck her hard and fast, and Kat strained against the building pleasure and followed suit. They stared into one another, writhing and fucking.

"I'm going over," Kat said.

Brynn smiled wickedly. "Yes, go. I want to watch you come all over me."

Kat reared back and came while calling to the ceiling. Brynn went seconds later, crying out for her, grabbing her face and kissing her hard and hungry. Kat kissed her back so desperate for her, all of her, she nearly swallowed her whole as she came into her hand, once, twice, then three times as they found engorged clits with their thumbs.

"Kat," Brynn cried, pulling her mouth away to nibble her jaw and bite into her neck.

"Fuck," Kat said as the sensation of her teeth sent one last wave of pleasure through her. "Oh, fuck, Brynn." They slowed and eventually stilled. Kat could feel her walls pulse around her fingers. Brynn fell into her, heaving for breath.

"You're beautiful," Brynn said. "That was so…"

"Fucking amazing?"

Brynn laughed. "Something like that."

Kat held the small of her back and kissed her softly. She licked the sweat from her neck. "You taste so good."

Brynn rested her cheek against Kat's chest. "Mm, so do you. I think I may have drawn blood on that last bite."

Kat laughed, feeling the throb on her neck. "I think you may have."

"I'm sorry, I just wanted to taste you so bad." She straightened and slowly retrieved her fingers from Kat's center. "And I couldn't wait for this." She placed her fingers against her lips and licked the glistening come, closing her eyes as she did so. Kat watched with bated breath, one hand lowering to Brynn's round ass, the other thrusting up in her once again.

Brynn smiled and sucked her fingers one by one. "Mm, yes. Just like that, baby, while I taste you. Make me come while I suck you off my fingers."

Kat groaned, completely overcome with desire. She thrust long and slow, getting off on Brynn's snaking tongue and whipping hips. When she could take it no more, she kissed her, licking herself off her fingers and plunging herself into her mouth. Brynn moaned and bucked harder, faster, clinging to the back of her head.

She came while they were fused at the mouth, and she lowered her wet fingers to stroke Kat once again, sending her over in a series of short, hard cries. Kat pulled her down and they shuddered into each other on the bed, lost in downy soft pillows and wet, hungry kisses. And before Brynn was finished coming, Kat turned her and lowered. She pumped her softly, easing out the last of the orgasm and then attached her hungry mouth to her, swirling with her eager tongue. Brynn screamed, called her name, and dug her nails into her scalp. She lifted her hips and circled them in tune with the rotation of her tongue.

"Kat, Kat, I love you. Oh God. Sergeant Vander, fuck me. Fuck me so good."

She writhed and tightened on Kat's fingers while her clit balled beneath her tongue.

"Make me come, baby. Make me come."

She came hard but softly, moving her hips in long waves against her. Her cries were sharp but softened as they fell, long and drawn out as she took as much as she could from Kat, fucking her fingers and face. When she began to shudder and jerk with aftershock, Kat licked her softly and watched as she came down, face heated with ecstasy, eyes closed like an angel, lips plump and full like her aching clit. She was the most beautiful thing she'd ever seen.

Kat eased from her and crawled up next to her, wrapping her in her arms. She nuzzled the back of her neck.

"I love you," she said. "Williams girl."

Brynn moaned softly. "I love you, Sergeant Vander."

"That's Investigator Vander, now."

Brynn turned and brushed hair from the moist skin of her face. "What? Really?"

Kat smiled.

"Is it—less dangerous?"

"Supposedly."

Brynn held her face. "Good." She smiled. "Oh, the fun I can have now, calling you investigator."

Kat laughed. "I can't wait."

"No?" She kissed her, and lowered herself to her neck to her chest, to hover just above her breast. "Have I mentioned that I like to bite?"

Kat squirmed. "Yes, but not my nipple."

Brynn held her down with surprising strength. Her eyes flashed dangerously. "Is that any way for an investigator to act?"

Kat stilled, her nipple puckered and hardened so badly she could feel it in her clit. Brynn snuck out her tongue and flicked it, causing her pussy to flood once again with arousal. Kat bit her lower lip as Brynn continued to tease her, first flicking then lightly sucking. Kat arched her back and rubbed herself against Brynn's penetrating thigh.

"Just little tiny bites," Brynn said, watching her.

Kat struggled, the anticipation killing her.

Brynn took her between her teeth and bit ever so slightly. Kat cried out and bucked her hips.

"Oh, you like it," Brynn said seductively. "Don't you? My big strong investigator likes her nipples teased with teeth."

Kat writhed beneath her, her clit hot and full once again. "Don't tell anyone," she said.

Brynn laughed. "Oh, your secret's safe with me." She lowered herself some more. Licked her from her navel down to her pussy, where she gently spread her legs. She licked her long and hard and Kat called out her name.

"Mm, so good." Brynn smiled. "Have I mentioned I like to bite?"

Kat sat up. "No, not my clit."

Brynn shoved her back down and thrust her tongue into her mouth again and again, claiming her dominance. "Stay," she said as she moved down once again. She opened her with a wicked grin and licked her hungrily, then slowed and flicked her full clit. And oh so gently, she took her clit between her teeth and squeezed. Kat bucked up into her and grabbed her head.

"Fucking shit," she breathed.

"You like it." She licked some more, from her opening back up to her clit where she bit again. "You really like it."

Kat felt like she was going to pop. "Fucking don't stop."

Brynn laughed and continued, this time licking in short circles, loving on her clit, bathing it with juices and saliva and then she bit down and sucked, bringing Kat up and over. Her head bobbed as she sucked her off and Kat writhed and snaked beneath her, tearing at her hair and head and then screaming out into the night.

Brynn finished her off with huge circular licks, causing her to nearly claw at the wall behind her. When she spasmed and tugged on her head to stop, Brynn crawled to her looking like a devil. She kissed her deeply and then bit her lower lip and laughed.

"The investigator and the vampire."

Kat held her close. "Somehow that sounds good."

"It does sound good." They entwined into one another and stared up at the ceiling.

"Are you happy?" Kat asked.

Brynn turned and stroked her face. "The happiest I've ever been."

"Me too."

"How do you really feel about the career thing? Or about maybe moving to the city with me?"

Brynn stared into her and then smiled through brimming tears. "I'm fine with it as long as you keep your promise."

"Promise?"

Brynn kissed her. "You know about doing it again and again."

Kat smiled. "That's a promise I can definitely keep."

"Well then, you better get started."

They laughed and fell into another kiss. Brynn mounted her and pushed herself up, teasing Kat's nipples as she writhed against her.

She felt so good.

So free.

Free to love.

The End

About the Author

Ronica Black lives in the desert southwest with her menagerie of animals and her menagerie of art. When she's not writing, she's still creating, whether that be drawing, painting, or woodworking. She loves long walks into the sunset, rescuing animals, anything pertaining to art, and spending time with those she loves. When she can, she enjoys returning to her roots in North Carolina, where she can sit on the front porch with her family, catch up on all the gossip, and enjoy a nice cold Cheerwine.

Ronica is a two-time Golden Literary Society winner and a three-time finalist for the Lambda Literary Award.

Books Available from Bold Strokes Books

A Lamentation of Swans by Valerie Bronwen. Ariel Montgomery returns to Sea Oats to try to save her broken marriage but soon finds herself also fighting to save her own life and catch a murderer. (978-1-62639-828-3)

Freedom to Love by Ronica Black. What happens when the woman who spent her lifetime worrying about caring for her family, finally finds the freedom to love without borders? (978-1-63555-001-6)

House of Fate by Barbara Ann Wright. Two women must throw off the lives they've known as a guardian and an assassin and save two rival houses before their secrets tear the galaxy apart. (978-1-62639-780-4)

Planning for Love by Erin Dutton. Could true love be the one thing that wedding coordinator Faith McKenna didn't plan for? (978-1-62639-954-9)

Sidebar by Carsen Taite. Judge Camille Avery and her clerk, attorney West Fallon, agree on little except their mutual attraction, but can their relationship and their careers survive a headline-grabbing case? (978-1-62639-752-1)

Sweet Boy and Wild One by T. L. Hayes. When Rachel Cole meets soulful singer Bobby Layton at an open mic, she is immediately in thrall. What she soon discovers will rock her world in ways she never imagined. (978-1-62639-963-1)

To Be Determined by Mardi Alexander and Laurie Eichler. Charlie Dickerson escapes her life in the US to rescue Australian wildlife with Pip Atkins, but can they save each other? (978-1-62639-946-4)

True Colors by Yolanda Wallace. Blogger Robby Rawlins plans to use First Daughter Taylor Crenshaw to get ahead, but she never planned on falling in love with her in the process. (978-1-62639-927-3)

Unexpected by Jenny Frame. When Dale McGuire falls for Rebecca Harper, the mother of the son she never knew she had, will Rebecca's troubled past stop them from making the family they both truly crave? (978-1-62639-942-6)

Canvas for Love by Charlotte Greene. When ghosts from Amelia's past threaten to undermine their relationship, Chloé must navigate the greatest romance of her life without losing sight of who she is. (978-1-62639-944-0)

Heart Stop by Radclyffe. Two women, one with a damaged body, the other a damaged spirit, challenge each other to dare to live again. (978-1-62639-899-3)

Repercussions by Jessica L. Webb. Someone planted information in Edie Black's brain and now they want it back, but with the protection of shy former soldier Skye Kenny, Edie has a chance at life and love. (978-1-62639-925-9)

Spark by Catherine Friend. Jamie's life is turned upside down when her consciousness travels back to 1560 and lands in the body of one of Queen Elizabeth I's ladies-in-waiting...or has she totally lost her grip on reality? (978-1-62639-930-3)

Taking Sides by Kathleen Knowles. When passion and politics collide, can love survive? (978-1-62639-876-4)

Thorns of the Past by Gun Brooke. Former cop Darcy Flynn's heart broke when her career on the force ended in disgrace, but perhaps saving Sabrina Hawk's life will mend it in more ways than one. (978-1-62639-857-3)

You Make Me Tremble by Karis Walsh. Seismologist Casey Radnor comes to the San Juan Islands to study an earthquake but finds her heart shaken by passion when she meets animal rescuer Iris Mallery. (978-1-62639-901-3)

Complications by MJ Williamz. Two women battle for the heart of one. (978-1-62639-769-9)

Crossing the Wide Forever by Missouri Vaun. As Cody Walsh and Lillie Ellis face the perils of the untamed West, they discover that love's uncharted frontier isn't for the weak in spirit or the faint of heart. (978-1-62639-851-1)

Fake It Till You Make It by M. Ullrich. Lies will lead to trouble, but can they lead to love? (978-1-62639-923-5)

Girls Next Door by Sandy Lowe and Stacia Seaman eds.. Best-selling romance authors tell it from the heart— sexy, romantic stories of falling for the girls next door. (978-1-62639-916-7)

Pursuit by Jackie D. The pursuit of the most dangerous terrorist in America will crack the lines of friendship and love, and not everyone will make it out under the weight of duty and service. (978-1-62639-903-7)

Shameless by Brit Ryder. Confident Emery Pearson knows exactly what she's looking for in a no-strings-attached hookup, but can a spontaneous interlude open her heart to more? (978-1-63555-006-1)

The Practitioner by Ronica Black. Sometimes love comes calling whether you're ready for it or not. (978-1-62639-948-8)

Unlikely Match by Fiona Riley. When an ambitious PR exec and her super-rich coding geek-girl client fall in love, they learn that giving something up may be the only way to have everything. (978-1-62639-891-7)

Where Love Leads by Erin McKenzie. A high school counselor and the mom of her new student bond in support of the troubled girl, never expecting deeper feelings to emerge, testing the boundaries of their relationship. (978-1-62639-991-4)

Forsaken Trust by Meredith Doench. When four women are murdered, Agent Luce Hansen must regain trust in her most valuable investigative tool—herself—to catch the killer. (978-1-62639-737-8)

Her Best Friend's Sister by Meghan O'Brien. For fifteen years, Claire Barker has nursed a massive crush on her best friend's older sister. What happens when all her wildest fantasies come true? (978-1-62639-861-0)

Letter of the Law by Carsen Taite. Will federal prosecutor Bianca Cruz take a chance at love with horse breeder Jade Vargas, whose dark family ties threaten everything Bianca has worked to protect—including her child? (978-1-62639-750-7)

New Life by Jan Gayle. Trigena and Karrie are having a baby, but the stress of becoming a mother and the impact on their relationship might be too much for Trigena. (978-1-62639-878-8)

Royal Rebel by Jenny Frame. Charity director Lennox King sees through the party girl image Princess Roza has cultivated, but will Lennox's past indiscretions and Roza's responsibilities make their love impossible? (978-1-62639-893-1)

Unbroken by Donna K. Ford. When Kayla and Jackie, two women with every reason to reject Happy Ever After, fall in love, will they have the courage to overcome their pasts and rewrite their stories? (978-1-62639-921-1)

Where the Light Glows by Dena Blake. Mel Thomas doesn't realize just how unhappy she is in her marriage until she meets Izzy Calabrese. Will she have the courage to overcome her insecurities and follow her heart? (978-1-62639-958-7)

Escape in Time by Robyn Nyx. Working in the past is hell on your future. (978-1-62639-855-9)

Forget-Me-Not by Kris Bryant. Is love worth walking away from the only life you've ever dreamed of? (978-1-62639-865-8)

Highland Fling by Anna Larner. On vacation in the Scottish Highlands, Eve Eddison falls for the enigmatic forestry officer Moira Burns, despite Eve's best friend's campaign to convince her that Moira will break her heart. (978-1-62639-853-5)

Phoenix Rising by Rebecca Harwell. As Storm's Quarry faces invasion from a powerful neighbor, a mysterious newcomer with powers equal to Nadya's challenges everything she believes about herself and her future. (978-1-62639-913-6)

Soul Survivor by I. Beacham. Sam and Joey have given up on hope, but when fate brings them together it gives them a chance to change each other's life and make dreams come true. (978-1-62639-882-5)

Strawberry Summer by Melissa Brayden. When Margaret Beringer's first love Courtney Carrington returns to their small town, she must grapple with their troubled past and fight the temptation for a very delicious future. (978-1-62639-867-2)

The Girl on the Edge of Summer by J.M. Redmann. Micky Knight accepts two cases, but neither is the easy investigation it appears. The past is never past—and young girls lead complicated, even dangerous lives. (978-1-62639-687-6)

Unknown Horizons by CJ Birch. The moment Lieutenant Alison Ash steps aboard the Persephone, she knows her life will never be the same. (978-1-62639-938-9)

boldstrokesbooks.com

Bold Strokes Books

Quality and Diversity in LGBTQ Literature

SCI-FI

E-BOOKS

MYSTERY

EROTICA

YOUNG ADULT

Romance

W·E·B·S·T·O·R·E
PRINT AND EBOOKS